What people are sa

Amity: Stories from the Heartland

Brent Bill's "stories from the heartland" are old-fashioned tales of small-town life in the twentieth century, warm and good-hearted and sometimes LOL funny. A good choice for fans of Jan Karon's Mitford novels.

— **Peggy Payne**, a *NY Times* Notable novelist, author of *Revelation* and others

The people and places in these stories resonated with me in much the same way my own family stories resonate. It is as if Brent Bill has peered into our collective past and told the stories of our ancestors, people who **are** ours but who we have not yet met. And he imparts the stories with such grace and kindness, conveying that, "Here we are. This is what we are made of. And it is good." I've not read stories like this since reading Wendell Berry.

— **Shawn Smucker**, author of *Light from Distant Stars*

These stories took me back to reading O. Henry and made me forget my angst of the day. If you could bottle these, the pharmaceutical industry would take a hit. "I'm stopping your Prozac and prescribing four Brent Bill stories each day and one O. Henry every two weeks."

— **Marcy Hawley**, Orange Frazer Press

It was Joan Didion who said, "We tell ourselves stories in order to live." In this visit to Amity, Brent Bill reminds us how, and why, to live. Poignant, humorous, winsome, and wise, this is Bill doing what he does best – going before us, shining the Light.–

— **Philip Gulley**, author of the Harmony series

A delightful collection of very varied stories grounded in the detail of everyday life in small town America. By turns comic and touching, its deceptively light touch reveals the deeper realities beneath seemingly humdrum events. How even in the dark times love, grace and redemption can prevail.
— **Jennifer Kavanagh**, author of *The Emancipation of B* and *The Silence Diaries*

These warm-hearted, sweetly nostalgic stories evoke a world that is resonant with hope and graciousness. Here are characters wrestling with their ambitions and desires, and finding goodness in unexpected places. The goodness is always offered up. In these stories, it's there for the taking.
— **Erin McGraw**, author of *Joy* and others

As I read Brent's stories, I kept sensing lines from Kristofferson's classic "Sunday Morning Coming Down" reminiscent of a lost time.
Clean as a breeze storytelling fills these pages, a gift because we so quickly forget what really matters.
— **John Blase**, author and poet

With deep emotion and subtlety, J. Brent Bill has built a rich world of fully imagined characters. This brilliant collection sits nicely next to Middle American classics *Winesburg, Ohio* and *Mrs. Bridge*.
— **Dan Hornsby**, author of *Via Negativa*

Amity

Stories from the Heartland

Also by J. Brent Bill

Hope and Witness in Dangerous Times: Lessons from the Quakers
on Blending Faith, Daily Life, and Activism
Beauty, Truth, Life, and Love: Finding an Abundant,
Good Life with God
Holy Silence: The Gift of Quaker Spirituality
Life Lessons from a Bad Quaker: A Humble Stumble Toward
Simplicity and Grace,
Finding God in the Verbs: Crafting a New Language of Prayer
(with Jenny Isbell)
Awaken Your Senses (with Beth Booram)
Sacred Compass: The Way of Spiritual Discernment
Mind the Light: Learning to See with Spiritual Eyes
Imagination and Spirit: A Contemporary Quaker Reader

Amity

Stories from the Heartland

J. Brent Bill

ROUNDFIRE
BOOKS

Winchester, UK
Washington, USA

JOHN HUNT PUBLISHING

First published by Roundfire Books, 2023
Roundfire Books is an imprint of John Hunt Publishing Ltd., No. 3 East St., Alresford,
Hampshire SO24 9EE, UK
office@jhpbooks.com
www.johnhuntpublishing.com
www.roundfire-books.com

For distributor details and how to order please visit the 'Ordering' section on our website.

Text copyright: J. Brent Bill 2021

ISBN: 978 1 80341 366 2
978 1 80341 367 9 (ebook)
Library of Congress Control Number: 2022918487

All rights reserved. Except for brief quotations in critical articles or reviews, no part of this book
may be reproduced in any manner without prior written permission from the publishers.

The rights of J. Brent Bill as author have been asserted in accordance with the Copyright, Designs
and Patents Act 1988.

A CIP catalogue record for this book is available from the British Library.

Design: Lapiz Digital Services

Printed and bound by CPI Group (UK) Ltd, Croydon, CR0 4YY
Printed in North America by CPI GPS partners

We operate a distinctive and ethical publishing philosophy in
all areas of our business, from our global network of authors to
production and worldwide distribution.

Contents

To the memory of John and JoAnn Bill – my first storytellers.

Some of my lies are true.
—Huey Lewis

Acknowledgements

I've been telling stories all my life. And my life has been filled with people who have, some like my family with reluctance at times, listened to them. This, though, is my first venture in publishing stories. In the same way I've been telling them for years, I've also been writing them for years. Now some of them are finding their way into print. I owe a great debt of gratitude to a number of friends and family who have made this possible.

First there is a group of friends who invested, literally, in bringing this book to publication. Each of the following contributed funds to make this project possible. I am humbled by their belief in this little book and me as writer:

Sue Agan, Jeffrey Alfred, Kevin and Nancy Armstrong, Ellysia Banks, Linda Bill, Olivia Branagan, Mary Lou and Steve Chappell, Sabrina Darnowsky, River Jordan, Gerlinde Lamer, Sarah Lookabill, Jay Marshall, Mary Ellen Nease, Jim and Elizabeth Newby, Jay Newlin, Jack and Katie Patterson, Peggy Payne, Larry Peers, Rachel Pia, Chip Pierson, John Porter, Traci Rhoades, Chelle Riendeau, Deborah Ryan, Danny Schweers, Donna Higgins Smith, Shawn Smucker, Brad Stocker, Lee Ann Swarm, and Nancy Whitt.

Next, I am especially grateful for the work my dear friend Donna Higgins Smith put into this project. Donna has long been a supporter of my writing and in this instance read multiple versions of this work, offering suggestions and edits.

So, I offer my deepest thanks to all these good people – and you dear reader, for picking up my offering of stories from the heartland.

A Trip to Amity

He fumed as he sat in the still garaged car, revving its engine in disgust. *One of these days I'm just going to leave her behind*, he thought, though he knew he never would. He'd thought that off and on for thirty years and hadn't left her yet. Still, there was some comfort in thinking that it was an option.

Finally, the door from the kitchen into the garage opened. A short gray-haired woman bustled out, then hustled back in, rushed back out, stuffing make-up into a shiny black purse and climbed into the car. "I'll put my face on while we drive," she said in a tiny, ashamed voice. "That way you can get going."

He grunted, put the black Ford in gear and backed quickly out the driveway, scaring the neighbor's cat's Sunday morning saunter across the concrete. He tore down the street and screeched around the corner. She held tight to the door handle. "We've plenty of time," she said softly.

"So you say," he snapped, staring straight out the windshield. "You always say that when you're making us run late." She had made them run late thousands of times over their marriage. Most of the time he laughed about it. He even told the two young men who married his daughters to get used to it; lateness was a family trait. Even their son inherited it. He did love his wife. He had from the moment he'd first set eyes on her thirty-five years earlier, when she was working with a youth group's money-making breakfast. He loved her this moment, too, though he was as aggravated as hell with her.

"Sorry," she said, turning her head and looking out her window, watching the houses rush by.

"Sorry doesn't make up the time we've lost. The service starts at 10:30, it's 9:45 now, we've got 30 miles of mostly two-lane to cover and I told you I wanted to leave at 9:30." His ears turned as red as his cheeks as impatience reached them.

"I'm sorry," she said to the window.

"Yes, you've been sorry for thirty years now," he tore on. "Instead of being sorry I wish you'd just get ready on schedule. I'd like you to have a little respect for my feelings, for the way I want to get places on time. It may not seem like much to you, but most people like their guest minister to be there when worship starts."

"I thought the service started at 11:00," she said softly. "I thought we had plenty of time."

"Well, it doesn't. It starts at 10:30 and that's why I kept asking if you were ready. But no, you just had to..."

"Sorry."

That was the last spoken by either of them. The only sound was the wind whistling by the windshield as they headed southeast out of Des Moines, picking up speed on State Road 5. After twenty minutes of silent rushing, he slowed, still glaring out the windshield into the morning sun, and turned on to S-23, heading for Palmyra. The sun warmed the car, and he cracked his window to let fresh air in. Maybe it would calm him.

"Do you want to turn on the air conditioner?" his wife asked.

"No, I do not," he growled. It was still morning. His Lutheran frugality meant he didn't need to use a luxury that would be greatly needed by noon on that July Sunday. He didn't want to do anything that would cool his anger, either. He liked keeping it banked, smoldering, just like the humid haze rising from the fields they sped by.

Reaching Palmyra, he turned west on Erbe and headed further into the country. Theirs was the only car on the road, rooster tails of dust rising slowly behind them. The road was rough and he had to slow. He fingered the window opener, glanced at the a/c knob, sighed, and lowered the window. The sweet smell of corn and beans baking in the summer sun swept into the car, the wind swirling around his black robe hanging behind him, its stoles flapping in the breeze. Fine powdered dirt, lifted by prairie winds, floated into the car, settling on his perspiring face and coating his robe. His wife didn't say anything, she just looked out the window, watching farmhouses and fields. He looked at the clock on the dashboard. 10:32. *Damn!*

"What?" she asked. He glared at her. He hadn't meant to speak, let alone curse. Dammit, it was all her fault. The outskirts of a small town loomed out of the haze ahead. According to the map tucked safely in the glovebox, it had to be Amity. "Amity, population 400" said the sign they passed, slowing as a white frame church surrounded by sedans and pickup trucks caught his sight. He pulled into the lot, found an empty spot, and parked. He jumped out, yanked open the back door, grabbed his robe off the hanger and began putting it on. His wife sat in the car, putting lipstick on. *Why hadn't she done that on the trip out?* He reached in the car, grabbed his Bible and sermon notebook off the back seat, slammed the car door, and left her sitting in the front seat. He looked at his watch as he stormed across the parking lot, stoles flapping behind him. 10:40. *Damn. Damn. Damn.*

He took the front steps two at time, something he hadn't done in years, yanked the door open and marched down the front aisle. The organist played Martin Luther's "From Depths of Woe I Cry to Thee." *Still on the prelude,* he thought. *They must have waited a few minutes for me. I hope she's on verse one.* The lay leader was the only one on the platform and watched his purposeful stride down the aisle. *Probably didn't think I was going to make it.* He mounted the platform and settled into a pulpit chair. It was a nice, small church, rather plain, and about half empty. *Today's Lutherans are too lazy to attend church.* He sighed and shook his head. The air conditioning felt good as it blew out of the vent above him. He leaned over, smiled ruefully, and whispered, "Sorry I'm late" to the lay leader. The man smiled back, a funny smile.

The organist smiled, too, and launched into another verse. He breathed easier. It was too much to hope she was on the second stanza. Probably the third. He hummed along, remembering the words:

Therefore my hope is in the Lord
And not in mine own merit
It rests upon His faithful Word
To them of contrite spirit
That He is merciful and just
This is my comfort and my trust
His help I wait with patience.

The words stung him deep in his soul. Feeling sheepish, he looked down and noticed how dusty his shoes were. He buffed them on the backs of his trouser legs, then picked up his sermon book and leafed through it, scanning the carefully prepared manuscript. He looked up, tilted his head, and noticed his wife entering the sanctuary. She accepted a bulletin from an usher and made her way down the aisle, found a seat by herself, and sat with her head bowed.

Thinking of the line "His help I wait with patience," his heart broke. He had been so mean to her. And there was no reason, no reason at all, other than his need to have things the way he liked to have them. A fine thing, he thought, for a minister of the gospel to be so hateful to his wife, especially while on his way to give a sermon. The organist pushed and pulled at the stops, increased the volume, and continued on her musical way.

What harm had her dallying caused? None. None now; none ever in all the years they'd been together. He was lucky to have found such a loving wife, one who put up with his many moods. He would tell her that after the service, as they headed back to Des Moines. *I'm sorry*, he thought, wishing she could hear him.

She looked up, eyes wide, staring straight at him. Had she heard his thoughts? She mouthed something. It wasn't "I love you." He was no lip reader, but he had picked those words off her mouth enough times to recognize them. His brow furrowed as he tried to make out what she was saying. He noticed someone else besides his wife looking at him; the lay leader. He turned to look, but the man turned away. *What did he want?* The blamed organist was still playing. He looked back to his wife, who was pointing at her bulletin. He went to look at his, but had forgotten to get one when he came in. He looked back at her and shrugged his shoulders. She mouthed her message with exaggerated movements. He leaned forward in the pulpit chair, as if getting closer might help convey her silent words to him. Nothing. He leaned closer, so much so that he almost fell out of the chair. She sighed, closed her eyes, grabbed the back of the pew in front of her, stood up and spoke.

"We're in the wrong church."

He sat back, stunned. He turned to the lay leader, who nodded in confirmation. Face burning brightly, he stood up, and with as much dignity as he could, stepped down off the platform, walked down the main aisle, paused by his wife, offered his arm, and together they went out of the building. Going down the front steps, she handed him her bulletin. "Amity Friends Church (Quaker)" it said. A young man, hustling up the walkway toward them looked at the woman and her robed escort. "Excuse me," she said, "could you tell us where the Amity Lutheran Church is?"

"Sure," said the man, pointing "It's a mile an a half that ways out T-66."

"Thank you," she said, leading her husband to the sedan. She started rummaging in her purse, but he placed his hand over hers, stopping her. They went around to her side, he unzipped his robe, fished his keys out of his pocket, unlocked her door and helped her in. Then he walked around to his side and climbed.

Ten forty-seven said the clock.

"That was the longest 7 minutes of my life," he said, starting the car, putting it in gear and heading west.

"We may as well go on out there. I'll apologize for going to the wrong church." Then he snickered. She chuckled. Soon a summer storm of laughter rained down on them so hard that he had trouble keeping the car on the road. A few minutes later they zigged into a lot next to a fine red brick church with a bright white steeple.

They parked next to a sign that said, "Amity Lutheran Church, Sunday School 10:00 a.m., Worship 11:00 a.m."

Ten fifty-three read the dashboard clock. They looked at the clock, the sign, each other and started giggling again. There was much he wanted to say. And she had some things to say, too. But they just sat and laughed. Cars and pickups joined theirs in the lot. Many congregants stared at them; two middle-aged folks, one in a black robe replete with stoles, laughing so hard their car shook.

At 11:05 they were alone in the parking lot. He wiped his eyes, climbed out of the car, zipped his robe, straightened his stoles, and picked up his Bible and sermon notes. Then he walked around the car, opened his wife's door, took her arm and headed slowly for the church.

Places to Go

I need to learn how to drive, Mrs. Henry thought sitting at her vanity, brushing her curly, brown hair. She often daydreamed about the places she would go if she could drive. Once it was places like Mexico, with its brown Spanish speaking people. Now she dreamt about driving to church. Her sister's. The supermarket. She sighed as she brushed her hair. *July 1934. Next month I will turn thirty. How can that be?* Looking at her reflection, she started. She leaned to look more closely. Her eyes widened and her mouth dropped in disbelief. Among the brown nested a strand of silver. *Silver*, she harrumphed, *don't kid yourself. That is gray.* She reached into her hair, found the offender, wrapped it around her finger, and gave a smart tug. Eyes watering, she leaned closer to make sure she'd pulled the right one. She had, but now noticed tiny wrinkles around her eyes. She'd not seen them before. Mrs. Henry sighed and leaned back. *What next? Eyeglasses? I am turning into my mother.* She shivered.

She was a twentieth-century woman. Mrs. Henry had always thought herself an independent woman. She thought back to the days before she became Mrs. Henry. When she was Lillian Shields. An excellent student, Lillian had gone against her father's wishes for her. Something none of her older sisters had dared do. He wanted her, like them, to marry after graduating from high school. Instead, she had taken a year of classes at Columbus Bible College. Upon her graduation, she worked as a salesclerk at the F. & R. Lazarus store downtown, riding a streetcar by herself. Once a week she taught a Bible study in a tenement in the Bottoms.

She kept up her self-reliant ways after she became Mrs. Henry. She still taught her Bible study. She tithed her household allowance and sent it to foreign missions. She raised her two children with spirit and thrift. But this inability to drive rankled deep in her soul, telling her she was not so independent as she thought.

She checked her reflection and a gray-haired, bespectacled, wrinkle-faced old woman looked back. She blinked. The image cleared. Mrs. Henry looked down at the gray hair wrapped around her finger. *I need to learn how to drive*, she thought fiercely.

She pushed herself up and made her way through the neat white house the Henry family lived in. It varied little from the other neat white houses on Columbus' west side. Mr. Henry rode the streetcar to the Pennsylvania Railroad's Yard A, where he drove steam locomotives around the vast, dirty complex. Unknown to Mr. Henry, Mrs. Henry had been going to the garage for the last year and pretending to drive while he was at work. Her children, Luke Junior and Esther, sometimes followed her into the garage. They enjoyed watching their mother going through her game of starting the car, signaling turns, and parallel parking. She learned all the hand signals and never mistook the brake pedal for the clutch. She memorized the operator's manual Mr. Henry kept in his rolltop desk. She knew it as well as she did the 23rd Psalm, the Lord's Prayer and John 3:16.

She strode through the kitchen, out the back door and down the wooden steps, the screen door ca-thwacking behind her. She marched across their tiny backyard to a bright white two-car, story and a half garage. It was a novelty in a neighborhood of one-stall sheds.

The garage was a magnificent affair that Mr. Henry built five years earlier. The garage, like Mr. Henry, was sturdy yet economical. Nothing was wasted. On the outside, everything lined up. Its white siding shone in the summer sun. Inside, while perfect and square, it was obviously constructed with salvaged lumber. The alley doors had been born as a box car's sliding doors. Mr. Henry figured that if God could save people, as Mrs. Henry said He could, then Mr. Henry could save lumber. He felt his family should be consistent in matters of grace and redemption. Many things were born-again into new life in their household. The inside of the garage was evidence of such rebirth.

Mrs. Henry found her husband sitting in his garage. It smelled of gasoline, fishing tackle, machine oil, packed dirt floor, dry wood studs and asphalt shingles baking in the sun. Husks of insects caught and dried by summer heat littered the windowsills. She was surprised he hadn't swept them up with the whiskbroom he cleaned out his car with after each trip. *Maybe he'll be needing glasses soon, too*, she thought.

Mr. Henry sat on the running board of his gleaming blue Ford Model A Tudor, cleaning pieces of its carburetor with an old toothbrush. Other parts soaked in a coffee can half full of gasoline resting on the dirt floor beneath his feet. He looked up when he heard her enter. He nodded, saying, "A clean car is a good running car."

She silently thanked him for giving her an opening. "It's interesting that you should say that, Mr. Henry," she began, "seeing as how I came out here to talk to you on something about the automobile."

Mr. Henry's shoulders tensed. He wondered if she was trying to corner him into taking the Ladies' Missionary Society on another one of their do-good trips. He concentrated on his work. "What might that be?" he said to the carburetor.

"It is just that I've been thinking," Mrs. Henry continued. Mr. Henry did not relax hearing that phrase, "that the time is right for me to learn how to drive." *Oh, that's all*, he thought, relieved. A sudden slackness came into his shoulders. He didn't say anything, so she filled the silence between them.

"I think it is important that I learn to drive in case there is an emergency," she said. "What if something should happen to one of the children? I'm out here on the edge of the Westside and you are all the way up in the north end. What if our party line is busy and I can't get through to call the yard office? Even if I get the office, they may not be able to reach you."

Mr. Henry sighed. He felt tightness returning to his shoulders. Mrs. Henry plowed on, "Another benefit to my learning how to drive, is that I can get myself and the children to Wednesday night prayer meeting if you are late. Which, Mr. Henry, you have been almost every Wednesday since we've been married. Why you would think..."

"That's ridiculous," Mr. Henry interrupted. "I've always been home in time to get you to your precious prayer meeting. Within five minutes or so of when it was supposed to start, anyhow. You've not missed mid-week prayer meeting since you were in diapers. Besides, do you know any other women who drive? No! None. It's not done."

Nothing was said for a few moments. He scrubbed his car parts and she contemplated the top of his hat. She noticed that his straw hat was getting as thin on top just as his hair was underneath it. He noticed that she was not speaking. He did not consider that silence a good sign. Finally, she broke the silence.

"As you should know by now, Mr. Henry, I don't care what other women do or do not do. Maybe I shall be seen as sort of a trailblazer for the rest of them. I do know this – I mean to learn how to drive. I think you should teach me. Beginning today."

Mr. Henry didn't argue the point. It would not have done any good if he had. He could never recall a time that she changed her mind once she'd made it. His only victory in this would be to keep silent for a while, as if his contemplation, real or imagined, would make any difference. Finally, some face saved, he muttered, "If you are determined."

"I am," she interrupted.

"Let me put this back on the engine. Then we'll see about teaching you to drive." He half turned, smiled and tipped his hat to her. Her heart swelled so that she almost went over and hugged him. Instead, she simply smiled and said, "Let me know when you are ready."

Mr. Henry called her one hour later. When she came into the garage, Mr. Henry noticed that she had changed into a nicer dress than the one she'd been wearing earlier. She had rouge on her cheeks and the scent of toilet water vainly competed with the garage smells. He smiled and shook his head as he leaned against his workbench, wiping his hands on a freshly oiled clean rag. Sunlight streamed in through the wide doors opened onto the alley. "The first thing," he said, "you need to know is what all the gauges and switches and levers are for." He straightened, walked over to the car, opened the door and helped her in. He leaned over her, tapping a glass faced dial in the middle. "This, Mrs. Henry," he said, "is..."

"The speedometer," she broke in. "This is the brake pedal, and this is the clutch, and this is the accelerator, and this is the gear shift." She ran down a list of all the car's controls.

Mr. Henry's eyebrows shot up. "Forget anything?" he asked.

"Yes, this switch up here is to turn on the windshield wipers should it be raining."

Mr. Henry laughed, walked around the car, and climbed in.

"Let's go, then," he said, settling in and lighting a cigarette. He took a long drag, dangled his arm outside the door and looked over at her. Mrs. Henry confidently started the engine and backed out. Everything was fine until she turned out of the alley onto Fremont Avenue. Another car came their way. She stomped on the accelerator instead of the brake and veered to the right, nearly hitting a boy walking to the corner store. He scrambled up over a picket fence and scowled at her from the safety of a stranger's yard. Mr. Henry quickly pulled his arm inside the car.

Things did not improve as their trip progressed. Mrs. Henry forgot her signals. She stalled the engine coming to a stop sign. She stalled it again easing out the clutch. A couple of drivers got tired of sitting behind her at the stop sign and went around the car. One glared at her and yelled, "Woman driver!" as he passed. It took ten tries to get moving. She drove over the curb at the corner of Broad and Richardson, almost running down an old man waiting for the bus. He shook his cane at them as they lurched down the street and back to their home.

"You missed 'em both," Mr. Henry observed, lighting another Camel. That was all he said as they lurched their way back to the garage. Pulling in, Mrs. Henry mistook the clutch pedal for the brake and slammed on the clutch. The engine raced freely and the car rolled into the garage wall. She yelped and let out the clutch, strangling the engine into silence.

"That's one way to save brake linings," Mr. Henry said, climbing out to inspect the bumper and wall. Mrs. Henry said nothing. She opened her door and headed out of the garage.

"That is enough for one week," she proclaimed over her shoulder. "Next week will be better."

But next week wasn't. Nor was the next week. She decided it was Mr. Henry's fault. She did fine while in the garage by herself. His presence made her nervous and forgetful. She decided to take the car out by herself on a day when Mr. Henry was out driving trains.

That day came one crisp autumn afternoon when Mrs. Henry needed some things from the grocery store. She decided that the little grocery store around the corner wouldn't do. She needed to go shopping at the gleaming new supermarket two miles away. She changed into one of her Sunday dresses and gathered her children. Together they trooped to the garage and climbed into the car.

She said a prayer and began the starting procedure she knew so well. She leaned down and turned on the gas valve under the dash on the passenger side. She pushed spark control to full retard and pulled the throttle lever on the steering column all the way down. Then she turned the carburetor rod and pulled it out slightly. *So far, so good*, she thought. *Now the moment of proof.* She took a deep breath, turned the key in the ignition, and mashed the starter button on the floor. The engine turned over once... twice... and fired. Trembling with the excitement of answered prayer and the backbeat of the four-cylinder engine, she proclaimed, "It is time to go."

"Mother, I don't think..." Luke Junior said.

"Hush up, young man. Your mother knows what she is doing," Mrs. Henry interrupted. She stared him down, daring him to backtalk her. He refused her dare. Satisfied, she eased in the choke, put the car in reverse and released the clutch while giving the engine a bit too much gas. The back tires spun on the dirt floor, found purchase and propelled the car backward. They would have ended up in the yard across the alley had it not been for the garage doors. They were closed. The Model A careened into them, knocking them off their hinges. They fell into the alley in a shower of dust and wood splinters. The impact dented the back bumper and stalled the engine.

"Damn," Mrs. Henry mumbled.

Luke Junior and Esther were used to Mrs. Henry's plain-speaking, but this was not the type they were used to. They sat expecting the sky to darken, lightning to flash about the heavens and the earth to open and swallow them car and all, sending them to the very punishment Mrs. Henry's word evoked. Silence in the auto and the heavens hung heavy.

"Ah, I mean, oh my," she said, glancing up toward a hopefully merciful Father. "Oh my, oh my, oh my." She climbed out of the car and looked over the damage. Then she reached in and put the car in neutral, while telling Luke Junior and Esther to get out.

"Children, come help me," she pleaded. Together they struggled to push the Model A back into the garage. She walked back to the dusty alley and looked at the now horizontal doors. Mrs. Henry decided they would look better vertical.

"Children, we have work to do," she said firmly. "We'll tell Mr. Henry about this little accident after he has had the chance to rest up after his hard day." After much grunting, groaning, shoving, lifting, and pulling, they propped the doors into place, leaning against the garage.

"Oh my, oh my, oh my," Mrs. Henry worried. "How will I ever explain this to your father? I will have to tell him the truth. Yes, that is what I must do. As soon as he comes home. Directly after his bath. Perhaps during supper. Maybe..." Her words trailed off as she and the children walked across the yard. She sent Luke Junior to the corner store to pick up the ingredients for Mr. Henry's favorite meal. She changed back into the dress she'd been wearing and then, when Luke Junior returned, busied herself preparing their supper.

Work in Yard A had been light. Mr. Henry got off fifteen minutes early. He caught his street cars home and climbed off at the Terrace Avenue stop. During the four-block walk home he realized he was down to his last Camel.

I'd best head over to the drugstore and pick up a carton, he thought. He ducked down the alley to get his car. Mr. Henry walked up to his garage, took hold of the door handles, gave a solid pull, and was buried alive.

Luke Junior and Esther were playing in the backyard when this happened. They hadn't heard their father coming down the alley but they had heard the doors fall and loud, but strangely muffled shouting.

"Mother!"

"Mom!"

"You'd better come quick – something's happened out back."

The three of them ran to the alley. There they found the garage doors flat in the alley and Mr. Henry's feet flailing beneath them. The doors barely moved for all his struggling. His frustrated shouting was so garbled by his lack of breath and the weight of the doors on top of him that they could barely understand him. They stood dumbstruck. Finally, they realized he was trying to yell, "Get these things off me!" At last they lifted a corner of the doors and he crawled out.

Mr. Henry sat up and glared accusingly at the children, especially Luke Junior. "Boy, is there anything you want to tell me?" he demanded.

"Not really, sir," said his son, glancing sideways at Mrs. Henry.

"Fine. Then let me put it another way," Mr. Henry growled. "Is there anything you *should* tell me?"

"Well..." said Luke Junior.

"Oh my, oh my, oh my," Mrs. Henry cut in, saving her son. "Mr. Henry, I have something perfectly terrible to tell you." She proceeded to plead guilty, but temporarily insane; or at least forgetful.

"Oh my, indeed," was all Mr. Henry said. Then he stood, propped the doors back up, dusted himself, walked into the house, and took his bath. When he came downstairs, he went directly to the front porch where he sat reading the *Dispatch* and slowly smoking his last Camel until supper was called.

"Father, we are grateful for Christ our Savior and this food which was provided by your bountiful hand," Mrs. Henry prayed at the dinner table. "Please bless it to our bodies and forgive us any trespasses against you."

"Such as trying to kill her husband," mumbled Luke Junior. He was heard by God – and everyone else around the table.

"Amen!" cried Mr. Henry, who began laughing. Luke Junior giggled and Esther joined in. Mrs. Henry looked nervous and then, relieved, began laughing, too, though not so loudly as the rest of them. And that was the last of that particular tension between them.

Mr. Henry walked the eight blocks to the drugstore after supper to buy more Camels. Mrs. Henry vowed to never swear again. And she didn't. She did, however, continue to make her almost daily trek to the garage – but only while Mr. Henry was at work and the children at school. She secretly memorized the controls and manuals of a succession of Chevrolets, Buicks, and Pontiacs as her wrinkles deepened and white hair replaced the gray and brown. She sat behind their steering wheels and pressed the pedals and adjusted the seat and the mirrors, always careful to put them back exactly where Mr. Henry had left them. She watched Luke Junior and Esther driving those very cars. And at night she often dreamed about the places she would go... if only she could drive.

The Sword of the Lord

Jack was a bus kid. That's what the other Sunday Schoolers called him, arriving weekly on bus number five, unlike them in their family cars with their dads and moms.

Bus five had a bright white Blue Bird school bus body sitting atop a new 1960 International truck chassis. Navy blue letters proclaiming "Hilltop Bible Church" down the sides and "Jesus Saves" on the back emergency door in addition to the white paint set it apart from its siblings in the service of the Columbus Public Schools.

Jerry Jenkins was the reason Jack was a bus kid. Jack and Jerry were best friends and sixth-grade classmates. Jerry went to Hilltop Bible Church, which was awarding prizes to its young members who brought the most visitors to Sunday School. The grand prize for boys was a trip to Cleveland to see a pro football game.

"You just hafta go once," Jerry said. "I mean, it's the Browns."

"Okay," Jack said. *I'll go once*, he thought. *Just once, though. Enough to help him get his prize.*

The next Saturday afternoon, he asked his parents if he could go to Sunday School the next day.

"You see, Jerry can win a trip to see Jim Brown and Lou Groza and the rest of them play if he gets the most fellas to come to Sunday School," Jack explained. "It's some sort of contest they're having. I just have to go once."

This surprised Jack's parents, but they said okay. "Just don't plan on us going with you," said his dad. Jack didn't come from church-going folk. Both his parents had jobs. His dad worked in a factory during the day and as a school custodian nights and Saturdays. His mom was a waitress at a family restaurant on Friday and Saturday evenings. Sunday was their day of rest.

It was Jack's day of reading comic books. Until Jerry Jenkins invited him to Sunday School, that is.

On that first Sunday morning, the bus pulled up at his house, tooting its horn. Jack boarded and slid across a shiny green seat. The oily scent of new vinyl filled his nose. He ran his hands over his worn blue jeans as the bus jerked and growled its way up through the gears. The knees weren't quite as blue as the rest of his pants, but he doubted it mattered. He was only going to help Jerry win tickets to the Browns. He looked out the window as they picked up speed, the tires singing a song learned from the bricks beneath them. Trees and parked cars made swishing sounds that floated in through the open windows as the bus passed. At the end of the street sat an old brick Methodist church. A few people walked slowly under the maples, oaks and elms forming a canopy over Richardson, heading there.

The bus turned, driving up and down the one-way streets of the Hilltop, stopping occasionally to pick up more kids. Dappled sunlight breaking through the cover of leaves gave way to bright sunshine as they moved from the older neighborhood to the westside suburban expanse. They passed through Georgian Heights and Holly Hill with gleaming new homes. They sat in silence, the only sounds the singing tires and wisps of a song whistled by the driver.

After twenty minutes they arrived at Jerry's church. Sitting in the middle of a huge lawn surrounded by new streets, short trees and split-level homes, it was a modern blond brick building, close to the ground, its roof sweeping up to the sky. A chrome cross pointed to heaven, glinting in the morning sun.

They trooped off the bus, following an acne-cursed teenager who called himself the "Bus Captain," and acted like God had appointed him to the post personally. They trooped into a large room, where men dressed in dark suits handed out small blue and white, spiral bound books emblazoned with "Youth Sings" on the cover.

The room was filled with people dressed up, the men in suits and ties, the women in dresses. Some of the ladies' heads sprouted hats. Many of the kids sitting with them were dressed as miniature versions of their parents. Jack spotted Jerry sitting with his folks. Jerry saw him and waved. Then Jerry turned around. Jack stood in the back trying to figure out what to do. The other bus riders swarmed around him, taking seats in rows where nobody else but them was sitting.

"C'mon kid," called the teenager, waving him forward, impatient, "c'mon and sit down." Jack went to where the rest of the bus kids sat and plopped down on a brown vinyl seated, steel framed chair, playing with the songbook.

A thin young man with heavy black framed glasses went up on the stage in front of the room. He blew into a microphone. "This is the day the Lord hath made," he proclaimed, as if this was a special revelation that had only come to him. "We will be glad and rejoice in it." Welcome to opening exercises. Let's take our song books and turn to page 36 and sing out on "He Lives." A lady with bluish gray hair started banging on a short blond piano.

Everybody rose from their seats and sang vigorously, just like the young man commanded. Jack read the words and acted like he was singing, wanting to fit in. But he didn't. He didn't have any idea what was going on. He wished he was back home with his comic books and his mom and dad upstairs in their bed.

They sang more songs; choruses with titles like "Heavenly Sunshine," "Every Day with Jesus," and one Jack liked called "Deep and Wide." It had motions and was easy to learn.

Then they took an offering. Jack didn't have any money with him. He didn't know he had to pay to get in. So, he faked it, reaching into the offering plate and rustling the money around like he was putting some in as it went by.

Then the song leader got up, blew into the microphone again, like it might have gotten switched off when he wasn't looking, and announced it was time for Sunday School. Jack thought that's where he'd been. Everybody got up and started leaving the room. Except Jack. He just stood there. He felt lost, wondering where to go. Jerry came to where Jack was standing.

"Follow me," he said. "I'll show you where class is. Our teacher is Mr. Lloyd. That's him up there," he said, pointing to a tall man walking ahead of them. Lloyd had shiny silver hair, slicked back and the scent of Old Spice trailed behind him as they walked down the long, concrete block hallway.

Mr. Lloyd stopped and turned to stand in the doorway of one of the rooms. "Hi, Mr. Lloyd," Jerry said. "This is my friend, Jack. I invited him to Sunday School." He beamed. "Make sure you count him!"

"That's five visitors this month," Lloyd said, writing something in a small white book. "You're in the lead so far for the tickets. Welcome to 'Boanerges,' Jack," Lloyd said, shaking Jack's hand. "That's what we call the sixth-grade boys' class. And why's that, men," Lloyd called over his shoulder.

"Boanerges. That was Jesus' nickname for two of his gang," said one of the boys sitting in the brightly painted classroom. "and he surnamed them Boanerges, which is, 'The sons of thunder.' That's from the Bible."

"That's a good nickname for this group, don't you agree?" Lloyd asked Jack, steering him into the room.

They didn't look too thundery to Jack, quietly seated around tables, each with slicked back hair and shimmering shined shoes like Lloyd's. Jack shuffled his feet, remembering the rough, scuffed toes of his brown oxfords. Even Jerry Jenkins was dressed nicer than he was. A lot nicer. Not like he was at school. And they all carried big black books, too.

One of them, Bobby Johnson, the kid who'd recited that thing he claimed was from a Bible, had a clip-on tie. "His dad owns the TV store in Great Western shopping center," Jerry whispered to

Jack as they sat down. Jack was impressed. Great Western had cool stores to look at stuff in, even if they couldn't afford much, and the "Walk O' Wonder" with miniature representations of Niagara Falls, the Eiffel Tower, the Sphinx, and more. It was a cool place to visit. As Jack looked around the room, he noticed Bobby's black book was the biggest of them all.

Mr. Lloyd rummaged around in a bookstand and found a shabby black book that he handed to Jack. "Holy Bible" was stamped in gold on the cover. Then he said, "Let's all look at one of my favorite stories. Take your Bibles and turn in the scriptures to 1 Samuel 17." The Bibles plopped down on the table, boys furiously fingering them, looking for Samuel. Except for Jack, who didn't have a clue where to begin.

"Here," said Jerry, who had already found it. "Let me help. It's toward the beginning."

While they were finding it, Lloyd began reading, "Now the Philistines gathered together their armies to battle, and were gathered together at Shochoh, which belongeth to Judah, and pitched between Shochoh and Azekah, in Ephes-dammim. And Saul and the men of Israel were gathered together, and pitched by the valley of Elah, and set the battle in array against the Philistines." He paused, "Now let's read around the room. You begin Bobby."

This is okay, thought Jack. *I didn't know we'd get to hear war stories.* As Bobby and the other boys read, he learned the story had a giant, too. Jack read, though he stumbled over *Ephrathite* and *Abinadab*. He loved the fact that the hero was a boy about his age. It was great how David took on the giant with nothing but a slingshot and some stones. And then chopped his head off with the giant's own sword.

When they finished reading the story, Mr. Lloyd announced, "It's time for a sword drill."

That sounded exciting to Jack, but he didn't see any weapons stacked in the corner.

"So where are the swords?" he asked. "Are they real?" The other boys laughed, except Jerry who gave them a look that was a mixture of *Lay off my friend* and *He can't help it*.

Mr. Lloyd chuckled and said, "They're as real as they get. Son, you've got one in your hands. 'For the word of God *is* quick, and powerful, and sharper than any two-edged sword, piercing even to the dividing asunder of soul and spirit, and of the joints and marrow, and *is* a discerner of the thoughts and intents of the heart.' Hebrews 4:12" He took the Bible, which Jack was already thinking of as his, and leafed through it, stopping at the verse he'd just said from memory. He showed it to Jack.

"You'll see what a sword drill is soon," he said. "Just do what the other soldiers of the Lord do."

The boys assembled ranks, as Mr. Lloyd told them to, lining up in a straight line, singing "I will never march in the infantry, ride in the cavalry, shoot the artillery, I will never fly o'er the enemy, 'cause' I'm in the Lord's Army, Yes, sir!" They snapped to attention; Bibles held in rigid right arms.

"Present arms," he barked. Christ's commandos raised their Bibles crisply, holding them out in front of them. Jack imitated them. "Ready," he snapped. "Aim – Daniel 3:25" The boys started rifling their Bibles. Bobby Johnson hollered out "Here, sir."

"Fire," Lloyd called.

"He answered and said, 'Lo, I see four men loose, walking in the midst of the fire, and they have no hurt; and the form of the fourth is like the Son of God,'" Johnson read out.

So it went for the next fifteen minutes. Lloyd called out Bible verses and the Lord's army searched for them. Most of the time Bobby Johnson was the first to find them. Then Lloyd said, "As you were." The boys took their seats. An annoying buzzer sounded and Lloyd lined them up and marched them to a big room he called a sanctuary for the 10:30 worship service. It had a lot of singing and some guy giving a boring talk. Jack looked in a folded piece of paper with typewriting on it that some guy in a suit had given him when he came in with the other boys. The talking was called a sermon. Jack guessed that was part of the price the boys had to pay for the fun of sword drills.

After the talk and some more singing, Jack stood in line to get on the bus and go home. Mr. Lloyd tapped him on the shoulder. He was holding the beat-up Bible Jack had used in class. "You can borrow this if you want," he said. "If you study, you may win a sword drill someday. Bobby's a tough guy to beat when it comes to the Bible, though. He's been the boys' champion since third grade." Jack thanked him and climbed on the bus. His parents didn't ask him anything about the day when he arrived home. Even about the Bible he carried.

Jack read that Bible daily. Sometimes he came across stories he liked, like Joshua knocking down Jericho's wall or people nailing other people to the ground with tent pegs. The *thees*, *thous* and *begats* baffled and bored him. He liked the books where things happened the best. He found the table of contents and began memorizing it, knowing it would help him in next Sunday's drill. He had already made up his mind to go back. His parents didn't object, his dad just repeated, "Don't plan on us going with you."

The next Saturday night he polished his school shoes and laid out his best pair of jeans and shirt to wear. The gleaming white bus arrived right at 8:45 the next morning. At Sunday School he won one of the sword drill rounds. He read more the next week. He won two rounds that week. Bobby Johnson, the TV store owner's kid, won five. He always stood there with his shiny loafers, pressed pants and clip on tie, looking like someone Jack wanted to be. Or smack. Jack couldn't decide which.

Jack kept improving. He sat in his room reciting the books of the Bible forward and backward. One time he'd do just the minor prophets. The next it was the letters of Paul. His folks still never asked much about Sunday School. He never said much.

Most Sundays they were still in bed when the bright bus pulled up in front of the house at 8:45.

The middle of October found Bobby and Jack neck in neck. Mr. Lloyd threw harder and harder challenges at them and seemed a little worried. One time Habakkuk. The next it was tiny 2 John. Or Micah or Malachi, seeing if they were paying attention. On the last Sunday of October, either Bobby or Jack won every challenge. The other boys never had a chance, not even Jerry, who rooted for Jack.

"I'm delighted," said Mr. Lloyd. "You boys really know your Bible. As a reward, I have a surprise for you. I've talked to Pastor Carmichael, and he approves of it. We're going to have a Bible sword drill in front of the whole church during the morning worship service. We're going to let you boys show your spiritual stuff in front of the whole congregation. It will be in two weeks. I expect you to heed the words of Paul to young Timothy – 'Study to show thyself approved unto God, a workman that needeth not to be ashamed, rightly dividing the word of truth.'"

Jack was nervous. It was one thing to go to Sunday School with the other boys and sit with Mr. Lloyd during church. But standing up in front of all those adults was something he wasn't sure he wanted to do. Jack looked at Bobby. He didn't look nervous. Then Mr. Lloyd said something that pushed Jack's fear to the background.

"I have a prize for the winner," he said, whipping something out from behind his back. It was a brand new, genuine leatherette covered Bible. Complete with a zippered enclosure, thumb-indexing, and gold leaf edged pages. "It has maps, a concordance, and a Bible dictionary, too. This goes to the winner of the drill. And his name will be embossed in gold on the front, too, right down here in the corner," Lloyd added, pointing with his finger. "'Know ye not that they which run in a race run all, but one receiveth the prize?' 1 Corinthians 9:24. Now, let the best boy win," he winked.

This was great. The chance to have his own Bible. A brand new one. Not an old one taken down from the bookshelves.

Jack was so excited he could hardly sit through church. Going up the bus steps later, he thought maybe he'd ask his folks to come watch. That night, at supper, he did.

"Uh, you know that Sunday School I've been going to?" he asked, knowing they did.

"Yes," his mother replied. Jack's dad looked down at his food, moving it with his fork.

"Well, they're going to have this contest..."

"I'm not going to be the door prize in some preacher's contest," his dad snapped. Jack's mother laid a calming hand on her husband's arm.

"No, it's not like that," Jack said. "I'm in the contest." He explained the Bible sword drills to them and told them how he was as good as Bobby Johnson, store owner's kid. And how there was going to be a Bible sword drill in front of the whole church.

"That's nice, son," said his mom, smiling.

"What's it got to do with us?" his father asked.

"I was kinda hoping you'd come watch me in it."

His dad's lips tightened. "I don't know," he said at last. "I'm not much one for church."

Jack's shoulders slumped, even though that's what he expected.

"We'll think about it," his mother said, giving his dad a look.

That was the last that was said about it.

On the Saturday before the sword drill, right before she went to work, Jack's mom came up to his room. She was carrying a hanger. On it was a new white shirt and freshly pressed pair of navy-blue slacks. "The Lazarus annex was having a sale," she said. Then she pulled out a new necktie. It was a grown-up one, not some clip-on. "Your dad can tie this for you tonight when he gets home. Shine your shoes."

Before he went to bed Jack hooked the tie his father had tied over the inside doorknob of his closet, so it would stay straight. It hung at attention over his freshly shined shoes.

Jack didn't get much sleep that night. The next morning, he got up early. He ate breakfast alone just like every other Sunday. Then he went and washed his face and brushed his teeth. Loud. *Maybe if I make enough noise, my folks will wake up. If they do, maybe they'll get dressed and go to church with me.* Jack stomped by their room on the way to his. He stopped at the door. Not a sound. He dressed and went back by their room. Still no sound. He went down to the front door. The old clock on the mantle chimed the three-quarter hour. Up rolled the bus, right on time. He slammed the door on his way out. As he took his seat on the bus, Jack looked up at their bedroom window. But no shade lifted, no face looked out.

The Sunday School hour passed slowly. There was no Bible sword drill that day, not even for practice. Then Boanerges lined up and marched to the sanctuary. The boys whose parents were regular attenders peeled off to sit with their parents. Jack went to sit with Mr. Lloyd. He scanned the congregation as they walked down the side aisle, hoping his folks had arrived, to surprise him. But they hadn't.

The choir came in. The pastor and his associates assembled across the altar. The song leader stepped forward and led them in "Showers of Blessings," "In My Heart There Rings a Melody," and "Since I Have Been Redeemed." The ushers came forward and took the morning offering. Jack dropped a dime in, taken from the bank on his dresser.

Then Pastor Carmichael went to the pulpit, a gleaming chrome and wood thing, emblazoned with a cross that looked like a jet about to take off, and announced, "Boanerges, our sixth-grade boys' class, under the able leadership of Mr. Clark Lloyd, has been learning the books of the Bible. Two boys have done especially well. One is Bobby Johnson," he beamed, "son of Art Johnson, one of our elders who recently donated the fine sound system we are enjoying in our new church today. The other boy is," he looked at some notes concealed in his palm, "Jack... um... Jack Andrews, who just started coming to our church. He's one of the children blessed by our bus ministry. Let's have them and their teacher come forward. Clark... boys."

As Bobby got out of his pew, his mother helped him into a new sports coat. Mr. Lloyd explained the Bible sword drill to the congregation, most nodding knowingly. The boys snapped to attention, Bibles rigid.

"This time, instead of waiting for the order to 'Fire,'" Lloyd said, "you may 'fire' at will, whenever you've found the verse." He paused. "Present arms," he commanded. "Ready," he snapped. "Aim – 1 John 3:17."

Jack was first. "But whoso hath this world's good, and seeth his brother have need, and shutteth up his bowels of compassion from him, how dwelleth the love of God in him?" he read. When he finished, he heard someone begin applauding. He'd never heard anyone clap in Hilltop Bible Church before. He looked out to see who it was and spotted his father, arm halted in mid-applause by Jack's mother grabbing it and the stern look on the faces of the congregation around him.

"Um, yes, very good, Jack," Mr. Lloyd said.

Then it was off for the next verse. They ranged through the whole Bible. Hebrews. Leviticus. Zephaniah. Revelation. Ezra. And on and on. Jack and Bobby traded off, neither one winning more than two challenges in a row. It was even at the end of 10 minutes. Reverend Carmichael coughed and shuffled his feet. He was ready to move on with the real business of the worship service – his sermon. Mr. Lloyd picked up on it.

"Well, we've time for one last verse. Whoever gets this one first, gets the new Bible." A pause. "Hezekiah 4:13."

Jack froze for a minute. *Hezekiah*. His mind blanked. Bobby wasn't moving, but he didn't look nervous. He looked confident.

Jack was sure Hezekiah was in the Old Testament. He knew that name. Was it one of the minor prophets? It didn't feel right, but not knowing what else to do, Jack opened his old Sunday School Bible and started rifling the pages. Bobby just stood there. He smiled. So did Mr. Lloyd. So did Pastor Carmichael. Even the few faces in the congregation Jack saw over the top of his flying pages looked happy.

Finally, Mr. Lloyd stepped up to the microphone. "You can stop now, Jack," he said smoothly. "That was just a little trick. There is no book of Hezekiah. Is there, Bobby?"

"No, sir," Bobby answered smugly, his smile as bright as his Brylcreemed hair. "That's why I just stood here. Hezekiah isn't a book of the Bible; he was one of the kings of Judah."

"That was a good tie-breaker, wasn't it folks," Mr. Lloyd purred. "Well, Bobby, you're the winner. Here's your new Bible." That was when Jack saw Bobby's name already printed on it. In gold.

They marched off the stage. Bobby went back to his parents, holding his prize aloft, to a chorus of "Amens" from the faithful. "Nice try," Mr. Lloyd whispered, as he went to steer Jack into the pew where they'd been sitting. "I told you Bobby'd be hard to beat." Jack wrested his shoulder from Mr. Lloyd's grasp and made his way around the back of the church and settled in next to his parents.

"We came in during the offering," his mother whispered. His dad didn't say anything. He just pulled Jack close to him, though he hadn't done that since Jack was six or seven. Jack put the old bookcase Bible in the pew rack, between the hymnals.

After a choir number, Pastor Carmichael went to the pulpit and opened the big Bible resting there. "Our scripture lesson today comes from the first chapter of the epistle of James," he intoned. "beginning with verse 21 through the end of the chapter." He read loud and slow.

"... and to keep himself unspotted from the world," he repeated the last verse, sonorously.

He looked up, prepared to preach. Jack's father moved Jack to the side, smoothed his pants and stood. His mother looking up in alarm.

"Excuse me, preacher," he said, so soft people craned to hear him. Even Pastor Carmichael leaned forward on the pulpit, as if to hear him better. "Excuse me," he said a louder, "but I wish you would have continued with what James said in his epistle."

"What's that, brother?" Rev. Carmichael asked.

"I wish you would have continued," Jack's father repeated. "I think the next portion has a lot to do with keeping unspotted from the world."

Rev. Carmichael and the rest of the leaders wore puzzled looks on their faces.

"My brethren," his father began, no Bible in front of him, "have not the faith of our Lord Jesus Christ, the Lord of glory, with respect of persons. For if there come unto your assembly a man with a gold ring, in goodly apparel, and there come in also a poor man in vile raiment; And ye have respect to him that weareth the gay clothing, and say unto him, Sit thou here in a good place; and say to the poor, Stand thou there, or sit here under my footstool: Are ye not then partial in yourselves, and are become judges of evil thoughts? Hearken, my beloved brethren, Hath not God chosen the poor of this world rich in faith, and heirs of the kingdom which he hath promised to them that love him? But ye have despised the poor."

He stood there a minute. "But ye have despised the poor," he repeated. Then he took Jack's mother's hand in one of his and Jack's hand in the other, lifting them out of their seats. He made his way to the main aisle and they marched out of the church.

"I used to go to Sunday School, too," Jack's dad said after they climbed into their 53 Chevy. He turned the key in the ignition. "I liked it. A lot. And I learned the Bible. I like it, too. A lot. But then... well, never mind, that's the past." He said nothing else. Jack sat with them in the front seat, his mom tight beside his father. They went to the restaurant she worked in and ate lunch. It was the first time Jack remembered eating out.

The next Sunday morning, when Jack went down to eat breakfast, his parents were already there. They had on the same good clothes they'd worn the week before. A plain cardboard box sat where his cereal bowl usually did. "What's that?" Jack asked.

His father shrugged. "Beat's me." Jack opened it. Inside sat a black leatherette Bible with a zipper and his name on it. In gold. His mom placed a bowl of cereal in front of him, as he looked at its maps, concordance, *and* Jesus' words in red. It was better than Bobby's.

"You'd better get dressed or we'll be late," said his father.

"For what," Jack asked.

"Sunday School," he said.

"I don't think I'm going anymore," Jack said.

"I didn't say you'd be late," his father said, "I said we'd be late. You want to use that new Bible, don't you? Get dressed."

Jack grabbed his new Bible, ran upstairs and got ready. When he came down the stairs, his parents stood in their coats by the door. As his mother helped him into his, he noticed that his father was carrying a Bible, its pages tattered and torn.

They left the house at 8:42, holding hands and walking north toward Broad Street. A few minutes later, as they walked, Jack heard gears grinding and a church bus horn honking behind him. It was still honking when they went through the open doors of the old Methodist church.

The Funeral

Mrs. Henry came from the kitchen and picked up the phone sitting on the old desk in the dining room before it could ring a third time. "Yes, yes," she said, and then, looking concerned she turned to her husband who was sitting on the sofa in the living room reading the paper and smoking a Camel. "Luke, Luke, it's the long-distance operator. A person-to-person call from your brother Shirl. It must be important."

Must be important, indeed, Luke thought, as he put down the morning paper and stubbed out his cigarette. Long-distance, person-to-person calls cost a lot of money in 1958. He made his way quickly to the phone. She handed him the receiver. "This is Luke Henry."

"One moment, please." A click. Then, "Your party's on the line, sir."

"Luke?"

"Yep."

"This is Shirl. Your brother. From Milroy Center." Luke sighed. Shirl always had a way of stating the obvious.

"Yes, Shirl."

"I'm calling about our brother Farley." A pause.

"What about Farley," Luke asked.

"Well, he was in a car accident this morning."

"Was he hurt?"

"Yeah. Pretty bad."

"Well, how bad? Is he in the hospital?"

"Nope."

"Oh, is he home," said Luke, starting to feel a little relieved.

"Nope."

"Well, where is he?"

"He's at the mortuary."

"What?! Why didn't you just tell me he was dead?"

"I was trying to break it to you gently."

Shirl went on to explain in his laconic way that Farley had been on the way up the state road from Milroy Center to Marysville to his job at Nestle's. It wasn't dawn yet and very foggy, so he was going slow. Then had a flat. He pulled his black '42 Ford Fordor to the small shoulder. There was a deep ditch along the road so he couldn't get all the way off the road. The Ohio State Patrol figured he was in the process of getting the jack and spare out of the trunk, when a Union County Dairy Co-op tanker truck, because of the fog, didn't see the stopped car. It smashed into the Ford and Farley, pushing the car into the deep ditch and hurling Farley twenty-five feet through the air and into eternity. He was killed instantly.

"How's Izzy," Luke asked, stunned. Izzy was Farley's wife.

"Purty broke up. Me and Orrie are going over there now and then we're gonna take her up to the mortuary to make arrangements."

"Well, tell her that Lillian and I are thinking of her. Let me know what the arrangements are."

After he hung up, he filled in the details for his wife, who had only heard his side of the story. "Farley's dead," she sobbed.

"Yep. Good thing is that I'm on vacation from the railroad this week so going up there won't mean time off." Farley and Izzy's house was in the country near Milroy Center, about an hour's drive northwest of their house on the Hilltop in Columbus.

"Are you going up there today?"

"I feel like I should."

"Do you want me to go with you?"

"Sure."

So, instead of waiting for Shirl to call back with the funeral arrangements, they changed clothes and made the long drive up.

While visiting with Izzy, Shirl's wife, Orrie, and Shirl at Farley's house, some of Luke's sisters and brothers stopped by. They paid their respects and more than a tear or two was shed. It was Monday afternoon. The funeral was going to be on Wednesday. Closed casket ("His body was purty beat up," reported Shirl). As the afternoon sunlight began waning, Luke and Lillian decided to head back to Columbus. Luke announced they were leaving and the look on everyone's face said *Yes, that's best. You don't want to be out on a two-lane while it was dark. Look what happened to Farley.*

The Henrys stopped at a diner in Chuckery for a light supper. A special afternoon edition of the Marysville *Evening Journal-Tribune* laid on the counter. "Milroy Center Man Killed" proclaimed the headlines. The front page had full details and some photos of the accident. The paper reported that the truck driver told the sheriff's deputy that he never saw any car lights through the thick fog and that he had no idea a car was stalled until he hit it. The Union County sheriff said he'd never seen a car so completely demolished. A photo of the car confirmed his statement. Mercifully there were none of Farley's body. Mostly his mangled Ford and the tanker truck. Luke sighed and Lillian wept softly.

After supper, they made their way in silence until they reached home, Luke glancing occasionally at the sunset in his rearview mirror and Lillian watching the night coming and then enveloping them.

On Wednesday, after an early, quiet breakfast, Luke said to his wife, "We need to be on the road before 8. Calling starts at 9:30 and I want to be there before folks other than family show up."

"I'll be ready," Lillian replied.

Luke went down the basement to the shower stall he installed there so he could clean up after a day on the railroad. As he showered, he looked at his reflection in the little glass mirror hanging from the shower head. There he beheld a tallish bald man with blue eyes and gray stubble on his chin.

Fifty-nine, he thought. *How can that be? That means Farley was just fifty-five. My two kids are grown and now have kids of their own. Farley had three daughters and two little grandkids. Kids he would never see grow, graduate high school, get married. Won't sit on the porch and watch the sunset or going fishing out at Bart's farm anymore. Won't do any of the things I'm still looking forward to.*

Luke was a man of few words, so most people seemed to assume that he had few thoughts, as well. But that wasn't true. He just didn't feel the need to share what he was thinking with everybody. He continued his ruminations.

I wonder what Farley was thinking. Did he see any lights or hear the truck at all? I hope not. What can I say to his kids? To Izzy? I'm not ready for this. I'm the oldest so I figured I'd be first. Not Farley who was the youngest. He sighed as the water pelted off his body. *I hate this. Still, I'm still here. So far, that is. It'll probably be the Camels that get me. Not a milk truck. Poor Farley. Poor Izzy. Poor all of us.* He noticed that his face was wet, even though he hadn't put his head under the showerhead yet.

Luke stepped out of the shower, dried off, wrapped the towel around him, and headed through the house to their second-floor bedroom. Lillian had laid out his blue wool suit, a white shirt, and a black tie. Luke dressed, wiped off his black dress shoes with an old cloth and grabbed his black fedora. Then he picked up a couple of fresh packs of Camels. "Goin' for the car," he called to his wife, and headed down the stairs. His watch read 7:45.

Out the back door he went, heading for the garage where he kept his 1955 butterscotch and white two-tone Pontiac Star Chief. He'd installed an overhead door after an earlier mishap with the previous swinging doors. Up it went. He started the car, backed into the alley, and drove around to the front of the house. It was a sunny, but chilly late October morning, so he left the car running and turned on the heater.

As he climbed out of the Pontiac, Lillian came out the front door and down to the car. He opened her door and helped her in. Going around the car, he opened a back door, took off his suit coat, folded it, laid it on the bench seat and placed his hat on top. He climbed in the driver's seat and put the shiny car in gear.

At the stoplight at Richardson and Broad, he turned left and headed west on US 40. It would be the last four-lane highway for a while. Out of Columbus they went, through Rome, then turned north toward Hilliards. West out of Hilliards, then north again, passing through Amity on to Plain City. All two-lanes, without much traffic. There was no fog out here in the country, unlike a few days earlier.

As they drove, Luke smoked, knocking ashes into the pulled-out dash ash tray. He and Lillian talked about Farley. Lillian remarked on the first time she'd met him, almost forty-years earlier. Farley was a gangly seventeen-year-old when Luke brought his city girlfriend to meet the family. Luke was the only one of his siblings ever to leave the family farm outside of Milroy Center to move to Columbus.

Farley, Lillian remembered, was very shy and didn't say much back then. But then none of the Henry men were real talkers... unless they were huddled together outdoors. That June day Farley kept glancing at the pretty young woman with her store-bought dress. He never said anything, though, other than hello. He did have a twinkle in his eyes that spoke of someone who could be a rascal, she recalled.

Together they talked about Farley and Izzy's wedding, them staying with Luke and Lillian on their honeymoon. They could afford a trip to the city or a hotel, but not both. A few years later, the young couple fell onto some hard times and in the late '40s, Farley had to sell his little farm. He auctioned off their six cows, tractor and implements, combine, the wheat and oats in the barn, their Dodge truck, and the majority of their household goods. With the money from the auction, after paying the bills, they had just enough to move into a little house outside of

Milroy Center. He got the job at Nestlé and then farmed a little on the side when their finances improved.

Luke and Lillian reminisced about Henry family reunions at the Union Country fair grounds. The young men like Luke and Farley pitched horseshoes in the summer sun, while the old men sat in the shade of the shelter house and swapped stories. The really young men played softball. Luke remarked how he and his brothers were now the old men, their parents' generation having died off.

At 8:50, according to the Pontiac's dashboard's clicking clock, the Henrys pulled onto Milroy Center's main street, one block lined with merchant buildings on both sides and the Farmer's Bank anchoring the corner. Just past the flashing stop light and across the railroad tracks, Luke saw Burger's Mortuary, a large white Victorian. It was probably built by one of the men who got rich selling his land to the railroad that passed through town. He pulled around back to the parking lot, parked next to a big black Buick Roadmaster, turned off his car, and sighed.

As they walked up the steps to the wide front porch, the door opened, and they saw Bruce Burger there. Bruce was the heir apparent to the funeral home, following in his father's and grandfather's footsteps. Luke smiled a bit. He remembered stories on trips home about what a scamp Bruce was. Well, scamp was the nice word. Now he greeted them, all grown and looking it. Though there was a bit of imp in his eyes.

"Luke, Lillian," he said, nodding his head. "I was so sorry to hear of Farley's being killed that way. How awful. It has to be awfully hard on you." None of the cityfied funeral home talk for him – no "Farley's passing" or "in this time of loss" malarkey. Luke appreciated the heartfelt honest words.

Bruce led them into the main parlor. The windows were hung with heavy drapes, the room perfumed with the thick scent of floral arrangements. Even though it was morning, the room felt dark. At the front of the room was a catafalque with a simple steel casket atop it. At the head stood Izzy, dressed all in black, dabbing at her eyes with a handkerchief. The women around her – his two sisters, his sisters-in-law and Farley's two daughters – all had donned dark dresses. His brothers, like him, had on their best suits. Except for Bart. He was a bachelor farmer who never went to church or anyplace he felt needed a suit. He did have on new overalls, a white shirt buttoned up to the collar, and a rather worn old suitcoat. He had put some kind of polish on his work boots. Luke smiled slightly at Bart's dressing like a poor farmer when every other year he paid cash for a new Buick Roadmaster. Luke was sure that Bart's car was the one he had parked next to.

Luke and Lillian went to Izzy who collapsed into Luke's arms. "Oh, Luke, what am I going to do? I can't believe this happened." Luke's words failed him, so he just held her, patting her gently on the back, and murmuring, "There. There."

Lillian took her hand and said, "We will be here for you." She really didn't know what else to say either. And though she talked almost all the time (Luke had nicknamed her Gabby), she knew this was no time for words.

As the first mourners other than family arrived, Izzy composed herself. Luke and Lillian moved down the line. He hugged his sisters, Hilda and Viola, Shirl's wife, Orrie, and Bertha and Helen, Farley's daughters. *Those poor kids*, he thought, as they sobbed against him. Lillian stayed with the women and Luke made his way over to the brothers.

They all looked sad and a bit confused. And strange, all dressed up as they were. He shook each of their hands. Bart, Shirl, and Stanley. With their bald heads and thin builds, they all resembled their father at this age. They mumbled words like tragedy, shock, damn truck, and more. Then they formed a line as callers filed past. Most were long-time area residents who knew most of the Henry family. Others were co-workers from Nestlé. The minister from the Methodist church, who was doing the service introduced himself and commented on how sorry he was to hear of Farley's passing. Luke sighed. Not audibly, he hoped. He thought the reverend looked too young to really know how to preach a funeral. *What did this fresh scrubbed young man know about grief and sorrow?* The time passed more and more slowly as sadness and tears filled the room.

Up by the Henry brothers, after condolences where shared, most of the men coming through the line began to talk about how the crops had been that year, the yields they hope for, and their wish that the weather would hold until they got everything harvested. "I look to get 'bout 24 bushels an acre," Bart reported. The men nodded approvingly. Luke observed all nervous men, obviously uncomfortable in the surroundings and from being all dressed up. Luke noticed that more than one or two of them were missing a finger or two. Chester Hanley's left sleeve hung empty. He remembered how concerned they all were when he announced he was moving to Columbus to work on the Pennsylvania Railroad. A number of them worried about him taking on a job that was so dangerous. He stifled a small smile and wiggled all his fingers and his toes inside his dress shoes. Still, he enjoyed the ordinariness of the conversation. As if nothing horrid had happened.

At about 10:50, Bruce, in hushed tones, invited people to take their seats to prepare for the service. Slow organ music gently filled the room as Bruce brought in a portable pulpit. "Abide With Me." "Crossing the Bar." The organist even managed to make "Amazing Grace" sound like a dirge.

Rev. Williams came in and sat down in a chair near the head of the casket. He looked appropriately solemn, but kept putting a finger in his collar to stretch it. *Must've tied his tie too tight*, thought Luke. When the organist stopped, he took a deep breath and then walked to the pulpit. Opening a black service book, and clearing his throat, he began to read. "Dearly beloved," he said, even though he didn't know very many of the people in the room, "we are gathered..."

On and on he read, rarely lifting his head from his book and never making eye contact. He read a prayer. He read some scriptures, said some prayers. The only time he looked up, was when he reached for a glass of water resting on the pulpit ledge. He took a big drink, he swallowed, his eyes opened wide, and he sputtered and coughed a bit. But then he put his head back down and read. He did pull out a piece of paper from his book and read Farley's obituary, which everyone in the room had already read in the newspaper. That was all he said about Farley. Then he said a little prayer and sat down.

Bruce came in and in a caring tone said, "Ladies and gentlemen, this concludes our funeral. I invite you to stop by the family on your way out. If you are going to the cemetery for the graveside service, please return to your cars. As we drive make sure your headlights are on as we process." He nodded and moved the pulpit out. Rev. Williams followed him.

Many of the mourners came to speak to Izzy and make one last stop by the casket. Some patted it.

After the long procession to Oak Grove Cemetery and the graveside service, the family all climbed back into their cars and headed to the Milroy Center Methodist Church. They arrived around 2:00. The graveside service hadn't lasted long, but the visiting afterward had. They talked as they walked through the family gravestones there. Markers of their parents and grandparents. Generations sleeping under the sod together. Luke remembered some of the stories they had told and wondered which ones they had taken to their graves.

Back at the Methodist church, the family all trooped down to the basement fellowship hall and were greeted by the sight of a serving table laden with fried chicken, meatloaf, ham, corn, peas, green beans, casseroles, Jell-O salad, yeast rolls, and all sorts of pies and cakes. The church ladies, as church ladies always did, had prepared a veritable funeral feast. Grief deserved good food prepared with care. It said what words that came hard to many farm folk could not. The women murmured their condolences and began taking orders for lemonade, water, milk, or coffee. Luke and Lillian filled their plates and settled in next to Izzy and Luke's sisters.

The room soon was filled with the sounds of quiet conversations, church ladies bustling to refill drinks, chairs scraping on the concrete floor as they were pushed back to make for another trip to the table for more pie or ham or chicken. There were a few tears and a number of chuckles as stories of Farley made their rounds.

After he finished his meal, Luke excused himself and walked around the room, visiting with all the relatives gathered. He was now the head of the family, he supposed, given that his parents and their generation had all passed. He wondered how he had gotten so old as to assume that rank. But at least he had. Farley was now dead and Luke knew that, though he wasn't yet sixty, others of them would begin to join him in the great mystery. He sighed and wanted a Camel. But that wasn't possible here in the church basement. Or even outside on the church's lawn.

Then he remembered that there was an alley behind the church and heading for it walked quietly up the back steps and out in the brisk October coolness. He shivered a bit, but knew a cigarette would warm him up. He pulled his suit coat tight against his slender body. As he walked across the yard, he glanced at his watch. Four o'clock. The sun would be setting in a little more than an hour. The autumn light was gold and slanty. He turned into the alley to look for a place where he wouldn't be seen from the church yard. He chuckled, because there were his brothers and brother-in-law huddled behind a garage, all smoking.

Pulling out a pack of cigarettes from his coat pocket, Luke joined them. He shook a Camel loose, put it in his mouth, and leaned forward to light it from the cigar in Shirl's mouth.

Bart laughed a low laugh. Luke's eyebrows went up a bit in wonder. Bart said, "I was just thinkin' of Farley and his practical jokes. Like at the reunion a couple a years ago when he gave Shirl that loaded cigar."

"Blew up right in my face," muttered Shirl.

"You were mighty unhappy," Stanley said.

"Yep," agreed Shirl. "He really got me, though. Almost as bad as he got Bart that time."

"I remember that one," Luke said. "He was so pleased with himself, he even wrote me a letter and told me about it."

"Don't believe I know that story," said Ernie, Hilda's husband. Bart turned a bit red as Stanley started the story.

"Seems Farley was gonna head out to help Bart on the farm after he got off at Nestle's one afternoon. He called out and asked if Bart wanted anything from town. Bart said sure, would he pick up some sandwich spread at the butcher's. So Farley did. Bart was in the barn when Farley arrived, so Farley went in put the spread in a little bowl and covered it with tin foil and stuck it in the ice box. But then, evidently, he was feeling frisky and opened a can of dog food and scraped it into the container from the butcher's. He pushed the bowl with the tin foil back behind a milk bottle and put the container with the dog food up front."

"He went out to the barn and helped Bart with some chores there and then, as it started to get dark said he was going to head home and have supper with Izzy and the kids.

"Then, the next day, he called Bart to see if he needed any help that day. Bart said no. Farley asked him if he had picked up the right spread from the butcher. Bart said no, but that whatever he got was okay and he was so hungry after skipping lunch that he made two big sandwiches with it. Farley started laughing..."

"I shoulda known something was up," grumbled Bart. "That joker."

"… and told Bart what the 'sandwich spread' really was."

"I was so pissed I almost drove into Milroy Center to punch him in the nose," said Bart. "But he was laughing so much at the trick he'd pulled that it made me laugh, too. I never could come up with anything to get him on." His eyes became sad. "Guess I won't have a chance now."

"I think Farley played a trick today," said Ernie, the brother-in-law. They all looked at him quizzically. "Remember when the reverend drank his water and started sputtering?" They nodded.

"Well, Bruce Burger says that every funeral he does he asks the minister if he'd like a glass of water on the podium. And every time he asks Rev. Williams, he says, 'I'd prefer a glass of gin' and then the tee-totaler laughs at his little joke."

"I'll bet Bruce gets tired of that," said Shirl.

"He does, for sure," said Ernie. "Well, two days ago a grateful… um… client gave Bruce a bottle of Four Roses Gin…"

"Bruce didn't!" Luke laughed.

"Bruce did," said Ernie. They all burst out laughing.

"I'll give the reverend, even if he is a stuffed shirt, some credit for keeping it together and pressing on," said Shirl.

"Bruce said that Rev. Williams gave him what for in the hearse all the way to the cemetery," chuckled Ernie.

When their laughter died out along with the cigarettes, it grew quiet. The sun had gone behind some clouds and the air grew chillier. Luke looked at his watch. Going on five o'clock.

"Looks like rain is a comin'," said Shirl.

"Hope not," replied Bart. "I wanted to get some more beans in tomorrow."

"Getting late," Luke said.

The men headed back, unspeaking, into the church basement to collect their wives. They made their good byes and then, because Farley was the one dead and they weren't, they headed home, to prepare for tomorrow's chores.

Round Yon Virgin

"You know what Saturday is, don't you?" asked my dad. Of course I did. What twelve-year-old didn't? It was Christmas Eve. *It always fell on the 24th*, I thought, *why would my dad think 1960 might be some exception?* I sighed. Every kid I knew, even my dumb little sisters, had been counting the days until Christmas. Marking each passing day off the December calendar. *Stupid old guy. I hope I never get that way.* "Well, you know what that means, don't you?" Yes, I knew. Every Christmas Eve, my parents' Sunday School class would gather at the church so they and their kids and a few others from the church could go caroling. I knew, even though I was twelve now, I'd still be expected to go along.

I was. And I did. On Saturday, after a quick supper, there were about thirty so of us who gathered around dusk in the small, black-topped parking lot. It was cold and had snowed, so we were dressed warmly. I had on a plaid flannel shirt, corduroy pants, rubber boots, a heavy coat that was a hand-me-down from my older cousin Steve, and warm hat. I quickly left my folks and three younger sisters to hang out with my friends Craig and Danny. Pappy Rudolf, ("He doesn't look much like the red-nosed reindeer," giggled Danny, cracking us up) the Hi-Yo-Fo class's Sunday School teacher passed through the group, handing out mimeographed song sheets. It listed carols in the order we'd sing them. "Hark, the Herald Angels Sing," "Joy to the World," We Three Kings," "O Come, All Ye Faithful," "Deck the Halls," "Silent Night," and "We Wish You a Merry Christmas."

As my buddies and I looked the list over, we talked about our lyrics for the songs. "Hark, Harold the Angel Sing." Harold was one of my dad's friends. "We three kings of Orient are trying to smoke a loaded cigar (boom!)." "And make the nations prunes." "Deck us all with Boston Charlie, Walla Walla, Wash, an' Kalamazoo!", from the comic strip "Pogo." "Joy to the world, the Lord has gum." "We wish you a Merry Christmas and a sappy New Year," and "Round John Virgin." "We'll have to not sing 'em too loud," said Craig.

"Or better yet, don't sing them at all," said Pappy, who had sidled up behind us unbeknownst to us. "Behave!" he warned.

As we boarded the old school bus that now bore our church's name, Craig and Danny and I made a beeline to the seat by the backdoor. "Behave," my dad said, as we passed. I nodded.

Why were people always telling the three of us to behave?

The engine coughed and sputtered and finally groaned to life. After some grinding of gears, off we went, bouncing along on springs worn out by the many previous trips by school kids. We pulled out onto the main drag of our part of town.

Usually, if one of my dad's friends was driving, and I cajoled and wheedled enough, I got to sit on the steps beside the driver and look out the tiny windows in the folding door. But now that Danny and Craig were on the trip, I decided it would be more fun to sit with them. That way we could crouch on the cracked green vinyl seat and face out the back windows and make funny faces at the drivers behind us. Which we soon began to do.

"Boys," a male voice ahead of us growled. We didn't know whose, but it didn't matter. If one father from the Highland Young Folk class growled at you, it was the same as if yours had. We turned around and slumped in the seat.

"Hi-Yo-Fo, as if," snickered Craig. "A bunch of no-fun geezers calling themselves that."

"Yeah," snorted Danny, "it should be Hi-O-Fo for Highland Old Folks." We cracked up again at our wit.

We kept up with more jokes as we listened to the whine of the gears as Bill Black shifted up through them. A little fan mounted on the ceiling above his head tried desperately to clear the windows fogging up from the combination of warm bodies and cold night air. We watch the parked cars whiz by as we passed down city streets, seemingly inches from our noses. The bus filled with the sounds of children's laughter and adult story telling.

Down through the gears. A slow stop. We'd pulled up in front of one of the homes of a shut-in from the church. Danny's dad stood at the front of the bus. Even we had to admit that he had a pretty good voice for an old guy. He was going to be the song-leader for the night.

"Does everyone have their song sheets?" Lots of heads nodded. "Good," he continued, "we'll go up to the porch then. I'll ring the bell and when they come to the door, we'll start with the first song on the sheet." I looked at the sheet and saw that we mostly were to sing just one verse of each carol. We probably had a bunch of stops and so didn't need to sing every verse of every song.

Out we piled and headed to the porch. We weren't very orderly. After all, we were Quakers. Military precision was something pacifists like us don't do well. The assembled group sang our carols. Despite Danny's dad's best efforts at leading us, we sounded less like an angelic choir and more like... well, I couldn't think of what. Some voices rang out, whether on tune or not. Others were so low it seemed like they were just mouthing the words. "Make a joyful noise," says one of the Bible verses I had memorized in Sunday School. We were doing just that. We were joyful. And were noise. Craig, Danny, and I fractured the lyrics. We ended with a snappy version of "We Wish You a Merry Christmas." Then it was back to the bus and on to the next victim's house.

For all our silliness, Danny, Craig, and I enjoyed *those* stops almost as much as we enjoyed our jokes, riddles, and poking fun on the bus ride. The people we sang to, no matter how badly, enjoyed them too. One old man heard our fractured lyrics. At that house, my dad had steered the three of us to the front row, thinking we might behave better there. We did behave better, but we still sang our own crazy lyrics. Just more softly than usual. That old man must have had good hearing, because his face lit up with a smile and he looked right as us. Who knew old people had a sense of humor?

"What wonderful singing," he announced through the open door to our ragged Christmas choir. Then he looked directly at us. "I especially enjoyed you boys' interpretations," he chuckled. Dad glared at us, so we bowed our heads contritely as we went off the porch and walked down the sidewalk to the bus.

"One more stop," said Pappy. "Then it's back to the church for hot chocolate and cookies."

I didn't like that announcement. Not the part about the hot chocolate and cookies. I looked forward to them. But the last stop was always at the same place. A place I found scary.

The huge rambling stone and cedar shake-sided house where we were headed sat nestled among bare trees at the end of a long, winding driveway whose tiny iron bridge crossed a meandering creek. It was probably a pretty enough setting in the daylight, but it felt haunted. Not haunted like some house in a horror film, but haunted, nonetheless.

It was called The Quaker Rescue Home. I thought that was sort of a neat name. It conjured up all sorts of images of shipwrecks and drownings and lifeboats and courageous life savers. These mental pictures probably came as a result of years of singing gospel songs with lyrics such as "rescue the perishing, care for the dying, snatch them in pity from sin and the grave" and

Brightly beams our Father's mercy
From His lighthouse evermore,
But to us He gives the keeping
Of the lights along the shore.
Let the lower lights be burning!

Send a gleam across the wave!
Some poor fainting, struggling seaman
You may rescue, you may save.

But the Quaker Rescue Home had no "poor fainting, struggling seaman" or any other sorts of men in need of heroic efforts and superhuman rescue operations. Instead, it was a home for, as my dad told me, girls who had gotten in trouble.

Since I had three younger sisters, I was pretty sure I knew what trouble was. My sisters were no saints. Unlike me. But it was obvious the way everyone talked about the Quaker Rescue Home, that these girls were in a different kind of trouble. Serious trouble. I often wondered if they were hiding from the law or something, because the kind of trouble they had to be in must have been pretty bad.

After our previous year's caroling trip ended there, I finally worked up enough nerve to ask my mom about it. "Go talk to your dad," she said.

So I went to Dad. He squirmed a bit and turned red. Seemed like he didn't want to talk about it either. Finally, he explained that these young women were unwed mothers.

"What's so bad about that?"

"Well, you see, they are expecting babies and they're not married."

"How can that happen? You told me that when a man and a woman are married and they want to have children, then they come together in a special way and have a baby. If they're not married, how could they come together that way?"

He kinda looked toward Heaven as if he might get some help with this conversation. No such help was forthcoming.

"Usually," he started slowly, "being married is how it happens. Actually, though, a man and a woman don't have to be married to come together."

"Why would they do it then? If they don't want a baby?"

"Oh, son," he sighed. "one day soon you'll understand. You just need to know that you should never, ever come together with a girl like that until you're married. It's a sin. A very bad thing. And if she would ever, um, find herself expecting, her family would send her away to the rescue home to have her baby and give it up for adoption."

"So, what's it rescuing them from."

"From shame. And sin. They can find forgiveness there and maybe get saved."

I must have still looked bewildered because once again, as he often had, he pulled out his you'll understand when you're older line.

As we drove down the lamplit streets, a light snow started falling. The ride was fairly quiet. I really didn't understand the adults' unease but picked up on it quickly. Craig, Danny, and I sat quietly. No jokes now.

At last, we pulled off the street and headed up the winding drive, crossing the noisy iron bridge. Pulling up in front of the big house, Pappy said, "We're going to omit 'We Wish You a Merry Christmas' here. We'll end with 'Silent Night.'"

Slowly we filed off the bus. It was a solemn procession for normally what was a happy round of singing to come. Adults seemed nervous and shuffled their feet. Their kids stuck close to them. Danny, Craig, and I went to the back of the crowd. Pappy rang the doorbell. The huge wooden door opened and we entered a large living room filled with young women sitting on the mismatched chairs and sofas. A rather sad looking artificial Christmas tree stood in the corner and a few poinsettias sat on tables around the room. The faces of the girls didn't look like those of the other people we had just caroled to. They looked apprehensive. Sad. Many of the girls looked at the floor. Only a few made eye contact. I avoided making eye contact with them. Something was slightly sinister here.

Danny's dad stood in front of us and started us singing. We sang the same songs we'd been singing all evening. But they sounded different. Softer. Slower, despite his efforts to speed up our tempo. Less joyful. But we rushed from one song to the next, like we couldn't wait to get out of there. Which I knew I couldn't. Some of the girls looked up as we sang. Some even smiled a bit. But their smiles didn't quite reach their eyes. Finally, it was time for our last carol.

Silent night, holy night!
All is calm, all is bright.
Round yon Virgin, Mother and Child.
Holy infant so tender and mild,
Sleep in heavenly peace,
Sleep in heavenly peace.

When we finished, the girls, under the direction of the home's matron, stood and said thank you in unison. Then we walked quietly to the bus. Neither the girls who watched us board the bus or us seemed very joyful. When Bill Black turned the key and mashed the starter, the engine roared to life without its usual groaning. Even it seemed anxious to get us on our way.

I abandoned Craig and Danny for this leg of the trip. I sat with my dad. I noticed they were with their folks. I felt stained with something unexplainably dark and brooding. Especially as we passed down streets past houses festooned with Christmas lights, snowmen on the lawns, and manger scenes with smiling Marys and happy babies.

Ministration to the Sick

I hate seeing him like this, thought the Reverend Thomas Allain, walking down through the hospital's lobby. Visiting hospitals was part of his profession, bringing care, comfort, and a word of the Lord to the sick and dying. It was the hardest part of his ministry. He dreaded it. Not that he was uncaring. Rather it was that he never felt quite up to this part of his call. He worried that he would say something stupid or worse to people who had need of a good word. Allain felt much safer preparing sermons, administering sacraments, pastoral counseling, or teaching religious education. Anything but calling on people – especially in hospitals or nursing homes.

Still, in his twenty years as rector of St. Alban's Episcopal Church, the tall, thin, angular Anglican had been a regular visitor to many of the city's hospitals. Most of the time he shut out the antiseptic atmosphere along with his feelings of inadequacy. But not today. His brow was knit in worry. He knew he'd smell the smells and hear the asthmatic wheezing of respirators, beeping of monitors, and casual, quiet commentary by earnest doctors and nurses.

The old man he was coming to see had been a middle-aged vestryman when Allain came to St. Albans in 1965. Then a bank president in his mid-50s, he often stopped by and took the young clergyman to lunch, telling him tales. His voice was clear and commanding, his diction precise. He said things that Allain, his ears attuned to seminary theologizing, didn't hear until later remembering those stories.

Waiting in front of the bank of elevators, the smell of food from the basement cafeteria wafted up the elevator shaft. It lifted the corners of his thin lips as it reminded the priest of one of the old man's stories about the fortunes of war. The old man had been a young solider during the Second World War.

50

He and some of his men had taken a French farmhouse, chased its German occupiers down the cellar and then ate the breakfast the Germans had cooked. Allain's patrician face relaxed while remembering. He reached up and brushed a bothersome hank of gray hair back into place.

Soon a small somber group joined him in front of the elevator doors. They'd come to visit family and friends, he surmised. He scanned them quickly, looking for a parishioner among them or a friendly clergy face. Seeing none, he looked down at his shoes, shiny oxblood loafers gleaming along with the tile floor. A woman behind him choked on a cough. The doors opened. He punched five on the control panel on his way to the back of the elevator. He turned, leaned against the back wall and looked upward. People sneaked quick looks at the Visiting Clergy badge hanging from his blazer's breast pocket. As if the clerical collar didn't give him away. *They probably think I'm praying, looking up like this.* All he was doing was watching the numbers climb the display screen. *I don't want to disappoint them.* He patted his blazer, like a smoker looking for a pack of cigarettes, and felt it. His pocket version of the *Book of Common Prayer.* Feeling it safely tucked away, he prayed silently the prayer he knew he'd soon be praying aloud.

The Almighty Lord, who is a strong tower to all who put their trust in him, to whom all things in heaven, on earth, and under the earth bow and obey: Be now and ever more your defense, and make you know and feel that the only Name under heaven given for health and salvation is the Name of our Lord Jesus Christ. Amen, the "Amen" coming as the doors slid open. He excused himself and made his way out of the crowded car.

Walking down the hall, he thought how much he loved all his parishioners. God had given them to him and him to them when he was just a few years out of seminary. They had grown together. Now he was baptizing their children's children. And burying the older among them. In a week or two he'd be burying the old man he was going to see. While he loved all his parishioners, he felt that this old man got a larger share of love than some others did.

Allain slowed his walk, wishing the old man asleep. Then he could sit and pray; pretending that the once slender face now swollen with fluid and smelling of freshly washed decay was someone else's. When the priest poked his head in the room, he heard the nurse behind the curtain talking. The nurse pulled the curtain back with a rustle and said, her voice bright with false cheer, "It looks like we've got company."

"I do," the man in the bed groused, words slurred by painkillers, "don't know about you."

"Oh, you joker," she laughed, brushing the minister on her way out. "He's having a bad day," she whispered conspiratorially in Allain's ear.

"Hello, Father Tom," the old man said, blue eyes swimming in his bloated face. "Come to minister to the sick and dying?"

"Yes, sir," the minister answered, "and I've come to see you, too." He grimaced at his weak joke at the same time the old man did. Allain pulled a chair across the floor, scraping contrails across the freshly waxed surface. He noted new lines and tubes running from the old man to various machines strewn around his bed. "How are you feeling?"

"Like Hell," grimaced the old man. "Really. What they're pumping burns like Hades. Glad I'm a good Episcopalian. Don't have to worry about going there."

"I doubt you'd go there even if you weren't a good Episcopalian," Allain said. "You've been a good Christian. You've kept the faith. That's all that matters to God."

"Cheap grace if I ever heard it. Thought you learned better in seminary." Pain scrabbled across the old man's face. He shuddered, then took a deep breath.

"I did," replied Allain, willing the old man to focus on his words rather than his pain. "It was your stories that undid all that learning. They convinced me that grace was worse than cheap, that it was free. If my theology is wrong, then you are to blame."

"Did tell lots of stories," the old man grinned grotesquely, his teeth yellowed and gums shrunken from chemotherapy. His diction and grammar were both being affected by the chemo and the business of dying.

"You are full of them," agreed Allain.

"Favorite, Father Tom?"

"That's easy," said Allain, looking at the ceiling, remembering. "I thought about it just today, here in the hospital as I came to see you. It's the one you told every time you men put on the pancake breakfast raising funds for the parish school. You always talked about the time during the war that you and your men captured a farmhouse, chased the Germans down into the cellar and then ate the breakfast they'd been cooking." He laughed, hoping to whisk the old man back to the safety of the parish school kitchen. "That's still one of the best stories I've ever heard."

When he looked down he saw the old man wasn't smiling. His eyes were shut and hurt stole across his face. "More pain?" Allain asked, helpless. "Do you want me to get the nurse?"

"More pain," the man replied so softly Allain had trouble hearing him. "But not from damned cancer. It's... from remembering that day and the stupid story."

"I don't think it is stu..." Allain started to reply, wanting to reassure the old man.

"Because you don't know the whole story," the old man snapped, turning his head and glaring at the priest. "There's a lot you don't know," he coughed and turned his gaze to the ceiling. "Weren't there," resigned.

Allain stared at his shoes, not knowing where else to look.

"Was July '44," the old man began, his voice clearer than Allain had heard it in months. "Bingham's battalion got far as edge of St. Lô. Units of 11th Panzer division got behind them. Cut them off. They were in bad way. Men lived on candy bars 'cause that was all they had. Moving up one night, one of the squads coming to relieve them, we came on a farmhouse. It sat in a field between us and St. Lô. I suspected it was an observation post directing fire on Bingham."

"Was it?" Allain asked, amazed at both the stupidity of his question and the old man talking so much. His effort was obvious as the old man's breathing labored between phrases. Yet his voice gained strength with each word. His diction and command came back somewhat. He wanted to tell the old man to rest, to save the story for another visit. But he didn't.

"Yes. I knew we had to take it, even though we were down to eight men," the old man answered. "Our planes were grounded. Lousy weather. The Germans had nothing to fear... from the air. They pumped round after round into Bingham. Not much cover. Everything was blasted. We'd have to go right then if we wanted... to get there before dawn. To surprise any sleeping Germans."

"For something spur of the moment, it sounds well thought out to me," Allain said encouragingly, wanting to ease the old man's distress. He pivoted in the chair and leaned closer.

The old man's head shifted slightly on the pillow. He sighed. Taking a deep breath, he began again. "I stationed four of my men in a small woods. To cover us. Took three fellows with me and started across the field. The clouds broke. Moon came out. Bright and full. We got down and crawled through the mud. I would have prayed for clouds, but didn't seem right asking for something," he gasped "to help me kill somebody."

The old man's hospital bed made a sound like a small jet taking off; its tiny compressor redistributing air in its bladders. Allain leaned in even closer, amazed and frightened by the vehemence in the old man's voice.

"Clouds filled back in just before first light," the old man continued. "I breathed easier." Allain noticed both of their breathing easing. "We got to house as sky began lightening. Using hand signals and drawing in dirt, I showed my men where to go. I wanted to make sure nobody could back-shoot us."

The old man paused, gulping air, eyes squeezed shut. Allain wanted to say something. He searched his mind for a comforting word but couldn't find any. So, he recrossed his legs, examined the tassel on his loafer and waited. The old man's breathing steadied. He went on with his story.

"Before we took our positions, we heard wood thrown into stove inside. That meant someone was awake. Maybe they all were. Soon the smell of cooking came. It smelled good. Especially after what we'd been eating. I think we all thought same thing at the same time – *wait and let those guy cook breakfast. Then we'll take the house and eat it.* So we waited."

The old man stopped again, eyes screwed shut, pain pierced his face.

"You probably hadn't had a hot meal in a while," volunteered Allain, awestruck at the inanity of his comment. He flushed.

"True," the old man whispered, not opening his eyes. "K-rations are worse than hospital food. We settled and rested against side of the farmhouse. Gave him few minutes to get our meal ready. Then I tapped on watch and nodded. Corporal Crankshaw and I went around to the kitchen. Other two took the front. My plan was to take the cook and two coming through front door could... surprise the rest of Germans. If there were any."

"Which you did," said Allain, trying to understand why the old man was so upset. The story was unfolding just as he had heard it a hundred times.

"Everybody was surprised," the old man said, eyes wide, voice on fire. "Them. Us. We burst through the back door. Two guys went in the front. Cook wasn't in the kitchen, though," the old man spat. "He'd finished fixing breakfast. Gone to wake his buddies in front. He was walking down hall when my men came in through the front door. He picked up a rifle and fired – hit my first guy square in the face. Dropped him right there. I saw it as we came through the back." The old man paused, searching. "I'd tell you dead man's name, but I can't remember it," he said softly. Allain thought the old man's face held a look of betrayal. The old man looked at the ceiling as if he'd find the name written there. "Never mind. I'd never seen so much blood. Dropped him dead. The other guy, his name was Carl, fired. Killed the German. The noise woke the others. Luckily, they slept on the floor. The sight of Carl, Crankshaw, me, and the dead men in hallway kept them there. Carl hollered. He herded them up and then down the cellar stairs. Left them there, under their blankets. Crankshaw and I carried our dead guy, damn, what's his name... and laid him next to dead German. We covered them both... with a ratty curtain torn from window. Then we went into the kitchen to eat the breakfast the German cooked."

"I doubt you felt much like eating, though," Allain said, surprised by the violence and death that had been absent from the story all the years he'd been hearing it. He tried to imagine what the old man was feeling but was having trouble deciphering his own thoughts.

The old man didn't say anything for a moment, eyes faraway. "I did," he said, answering Allain's questions. "I hadn't counted on anybody dying, but I was still hungry. George... that's his name... was dead. German was dead. We weren't. We were hungry. The cooking smells mixed with gunpowder and blood... a horrible smell."

"You couldn't help that," Allain comforted the old man and himself. "You didn't know what would happen."

"Listen, Father. Listen well," the old man shot at him, with as much strength as his failing body allowed. "I should have known. That's why the Army made me a sergeant. That's why God made you a priest. A leader has to see what might happen.

I just got greedy like the rest of them. Greedy, hungry and too smart to see. Be careful you don't get so smart."

He paused, trying to take a deep breath. Instead of going to his toes it stopped right around his larynx. Suffering passed again across his face.

"It's a powerful tale," Allain said, trying again to take the old man's mind off his distress. "More powerful than the way you used to tell it."

"Powerful?" the old man snorted. "How is story of stupidity and two dead men powerful?" The pain front went through, and a slight calm settled.

"I understand," Allain replied, though he didn't, his voice becoming distant, professionally pastoral.

"Like hell you do, Father," the old man sputtered. "Don't go ministerial on me. We know each other too well." He paused again for breath. "We sat down to eat. Then Carl's head disappeared. The sound of train roared through the room."

"His head blew off?" Allain said, eyes wide open, horrified at the image and the inanity of his comment.

"88 round from Tiger tank," the old man answered, shaking his head, awe in his eyes. "Never could hear an 88 coming. Not like other shells. I looked out a hole in the wall and saw the tank, its barrel still smoking. Lining up for a second shot. I had to get Crankshaw and me out of the house before the tank brought it down. Heard its treads clanking as it came across the field."

The old man stopped, sucking air. Allain sat silent, his heart's urging to keep quiet finally overpowering his mind's need to fill the pauses with pastoral patter.

"I pushed Crankshaw toward door," he said, urgency filling his voice. "It faced away from the tank and was our only chance. We'd made it halfway to the woods when the Tiger came around house. My men set up covering fire – trying to draw attention. We ran fast as we could. The field was muddy, rutted. The woods got closer. I heard bullets whining off the tank's side. A bazooka shell hit its treads. It quit moving."

I didn't think a bazooka could stop a tank, Allain thought, keeping still.

"A bazooka can't stop a Tiger," the old man replied, resignedly, as if reading the priest's mind. "I knew why they stopped when I heard the tank's machine gun open up. They stopped so the machine gunner would have a clean shot. No sense wasting a main shell on two soldiers in open. Bullets raced across field, trying to catch us. Clods of mud exploded."

Allain closed his eyes, as did the old man. The story poured forth, the old man not pausing for breath, voice alive and scared.

"Twenty yards. I moved left. Bullets sizzled. Then right. I slowed. My men quit firing. Stood. Waving us home from behind the trees. Ten yards. My lungs bursting; sucking in air. Then something hit me. Hard. In my shoulder. It threw me into the thicket. Machine gun raked the trees and brush. My men ducked and grabbed me at the same time, pulled me deeper into the woods. The tank backed up, heading for the farmhouse."

The old man's eyes shot open, afraid, as if seeing it for the first time. The beeping in the room intensified. A nurse with worry-knit brows bustled into the room, examined a monitor, pulled out a stethoscope and bent over the old man. He pushed her away. Hard. She looked at him, eyes wide in alarm.

"Get out of here," he growled. She just stood there. "Now," he yelled, pushing himself up. She rushed out, heading toward the nurses' station. He laid back down and breathed deep. The beeping slowed.

"I passed out in the woods. My belly was full; but my blood level was low. That's the real breakfast story."

A doctor with mussed hair and starched white coat edged into the room, the nervous nurse close behind. The doctor studied the monitors, reviewed the chart, looked back at the monitors and said to the silent priest, though not looking at him, "Reverend, I hope you're about finished here. Our patient needs some rest." He took a syringe from the nurse, stuck it into one of the IV lines, and pushed the plunger.

"Doctor, for a change I agree with your diagnosis," the old man said, his words coming more slowly. "Time for Father Allain to leave." Allain stood up, still silent, discomfited by the story and the old man calling him Father Allain. He always called him Father Tom. For twenty years.

He headed to the door.

"Forget something, Father Allain?" the old man queried, morphine muddying his speech. The priest turned, puzzled. "Prayer for the sick?"

Allain reached into his coat pocket and pulled out the BCP. It fell open, well-worn after twenty years of hospital visits, just like the minister carrying it. He took the old man's right hand in his.

"The Almighty Lord, who is a strong tower to all who put their trust in him," Allain prayed, "to whom all things in heaven, on earth, and under the earth bow and obey: Be now and ever more your defense, and make you know and feel that the only Name under heaven given for health and salvation is the Name of our Lord Jesus Christ. Amen."

He went to withdraw his hand, but the old man held on. Stillness, in spite of the beeping and sound of the impatient doctor's shuffling feet, descended on the room. At last, the old man gave the priest's hand a weak squeeze. "Thanks," he slurred, closing his eyes. Then, softly, "Forgive."

"Pardon?" Allain asked, leaning in to hear the old man.

"Forgive," came the words, even softer. Allain wasn't sure whether the old man was asking for forgiveness or extending it. Allain let go of the old man's hand and started flipping through the BCP. The old man's eyes closed, his mouth fell open and he began snoring.

"He's asleep," the doctor said. "I gave him something to help him rest."

Allain nodded and put the prayer book back in his pocket. "Almighty God have mercy on you, forgive you all your sins through our Lord Jesus Christ, strengthen you in all goodness, and by the power of the Holy Spirit keep you in eternal life. Amen," he prayed as he made his way to the door and then down the hall.

The Crossing

I am driving fast along the blacktop ribbon that cuts through the Midwest farmland that my friend Donald calls "God's Own." Donald's a man of slow words and a slight drawl, so it comes out "God's Zone." His thoughts do not gush out of his mouth like some people's do. They trickle out one by one, like a persistent leaky faucet. I have to pay attention or I'll miss one or two of the drops and his meaning will be lost. Donald's a farmer and the cadence of his speaking matches that of the gentle risings and fallings of the land he makes his living on.

"God had farmers in mind when he made this part of Indiana," Donald says. "Look out there. Finest topsoil a man could want. Miles of rows. Some creeks and small ridges, but no deep valleys or tilting hillsides you'd have to maneuver your tractor and planter around. It's pick your spot on the horizon and drive to it. Once you've driven far enough, turn around and head back. Yep, it's God Zone, alright. Laid out by a farmer for farmers."

It doesn't look much like God Zone today. It snowed quite a bit a week ago and has been so cold since that the snow is still there. Fortunately, all of last spring's plantings of soybeans or corn have long been picked and stored. The wind shifts and shapes the snow, sculpting a sort of white Saharan landscape. I almost expect to see a tribe of Bedouin trekking across the pale dunes. They and their camels would have to be bundled up like Eskimos, though, to beat this cold.

The snow is so white that it seems to bleach the sky of its color. The sun shines wanly in a pallid blue sky. Remainders of corn stalks push up through the snow, like whiskery stubble on an old man's mis-shaven face. The shadows are deep and the snow is glaring.

The wind whips across the unbroken miles of fields, gathering speed as it howls along. I pick up speed, too, like the wind. Only I'm pushing against it. Dublin Pike is a short cut home and I'm in a hurry. It's been a long day teaching classes at the college in Richmond and I'm ready for a chair by the fireplace and glass of scotch.

Fifty miles an hour. Then sixty. Soon seventy. I'm grateful for the Henry County road crew that cleaned the pike. Some wisps of snow drift across, but there's no ice to be wary of. The wind pushes at the car. It's ten degrees out and the windchill makes it feel like zero out there. Inside, the heater turned up, it's nice and warm though. I'm grateful not to be out in that swirling Arctic air.

There's not much to look at. A few farmhouses sit in the snow, white on white. Fence posts poke up through the snow as if to take a look around. If they see their shadows will winter last longer? In the distance are patches of woods and a small-town skyline – two grain elevators and a water tower. You have to watch the road on a day like today.

Most roads around here are good and straight, laid out in mile square patterns established long ago. Dublin Pike is an anomaly. It's not straight in very many places. It's a winding old road that twists and turns along a little creek and where old woodlands used to be. It connects Dublin on the old National Road to where I live in New Castle and runs through two or three small burgs on the way. Dublin Pike was a mud road when it was first built. It carried horse drawn wagons filled with orchard apples and field corn to market. Now it's black top and tractors, combines, cars, pick-ups, and semis run its route at speeds the old farmers in their wagons could scarcely imagine.

Summer is not always friendly to Dublin Pike travelers. The only time I know when the county highway crew has been out filling in cracks in the black is when I hear the pop of fresh tar under my tires. I curse the highway crew and the specks of tar that will coat my rocker panels. On those days, in the evening, I'll have to park the car in the driveway and sit with a kerosene-soaked rag, wiping the tar off.

Not today though. Would that it were summer. There's no fresh chip and seal to worry about, but there is snow. The wind is trying to push me off into the duned ditches. It has a co-conspirator in the snow. The snow tells the wind, "Pick me up. Blow me across. I'll freeze fast and he'll slide on me." The wind agrees with this plan and blows little ghosts of snow waif-like across the road, in ever changing, hypnotic patterns. A light hand and firm grip on the steering wheel are called for. Back and forth the road winds. I'm winding with it.

The Indy 500 is run sixty-six miles from here each May and I'm driving as if the Dublin Pike was part of that track. Swooping low into the corners, high coming out of the turns. It would be easier to keep turning left, like in the race, and the wind and snow are coaxing me to do that. The road chooses to go another way and I must follow, back to the right. Then left again, around the big bend just north of New Lisbon. The name on our town's water tower is almost close enough to read now. The sun glints low across the hood and I squint to see the road. A long straight-away, a big turn and another long straight-away into town.

I slow down. The speed limit through town is forty. It feels like crawling. Then I'm out onto the open road and push down the accelerator. Soon the speedometer tickles seventy-five. I check the mirror to make sure the county sheriff isn't ready to escort me to the side of the road. All clear. I have to slow down to go over the railroad tracks ahead, but that's all. They're safe at fifty-five. I'll have to slow down. But off to my right, across the fields, I spy a train coming. A long one. Three gleaming black Norfolk and Southern engines with white stallions pawing the sky painted on their sides are pulling coal cars, box cars, autoracks, and intermodals stacked with shipping containers.

Why today? Why now? I'm tired and almost home. Maybe if I hold my speed, I can beat him. He's still a ways off. The warning lights haven't started... oh, they just came on. Still, I'm at seventy now and if the tracks are fine at fifty-five, wouldn't they be okay at seventy?

I shoot a sideways glance at the train. I sigh. I'll be here all day if I stop. Fifteen minutes at least, maybe twenty or more if he has to stop, back up, and drop a car or pick up one in New Lisbon. The engines are dieseling along, puffs of exhaust hanging above them in the cold and then being whisked into oblivion by the howling wind. The horn sounds as he tries to warn me off. I barely hear it over the whistling of the wind and the sound of my tires on the black top. I can make it. I keep my foot steady on the accelerator and eyes fixed ahead.

I hit the crossing flying, soaring over the tracks as the car catapults up the roadbed ramp leading to them. The warning lights are flashing, lighting up the inside of the car with an alternating red glow, and the warning bell is clanging. The sound of the horn blasts through the closed side window as I sail in front of the train. The car lands hard and slips a little on the snow and ice on the other side. The train roars by behind me. As I work the wheel to correct the little bit of skid, I see something out of the corner of my eye. It's my right rear hubcap, jarred loose by the landing, bouncing down the road, heading for the safety of a snow blanket in the ditch. I swear under my breath and stop the car.

The train presses on, its patient progress persistent. The ground shudders as it passes, as if from tiny earthquakes. I put the car in reverse and back up, mumbling and growling as I try to spot where the hubcap is hiding. Finally, I see an edge of it peeking out from the snow filled ditch. I should put my coat and hat on. I don't plan on being out long, but wind chill's at zero. I reach over to the passenger seat and grab the coat. I mash my hat as low as it will go. Open goes the door, on goes the coat as I stand up. I zip it up and pull on my gloves. The wind, happy to have me outside, tries to steal my hat. My ears feel as if they've freeze dried.

Now where is that hubcap? There it is. I reach down carefully. I don't want to fall face first into the ditch, though it would serve me right for having been in such a hurry. I pull the hubcap free from the snow and turn back to the car. Something catches my eye.

It's a short wooden cross, about fifteen feet away, back toward the tracks. It sits white in the snow, its paint peeling. A bunch of wind-whipped plastic flowers shudders at its base, a faded pink ribbon wrapped around the cross flutters in the wind. It looks as if it's been there a long time. I don't remember seeing it before. But then I'm usually rushing to or from teaching and probably don't see a lot of things along the pike. I know what it means, though. Someone didn't beat the train. There on the flat farmland a steady rhythmed freight train had ushered someone into another sort of God Zone.

My need to know who and when overpowers my desire for warmth, but I don't know why. I wander back to take a look. The name and date have been worn away by the elements. Just specks of black paint where they were are all that remain. Now there is only the paint peeled cross, the ribbon, and the fading plastic flowers.

The wind stings my eyes and they water. My feet are getting cold and urge me back to the car. My heart says be still. Just stand here. I feel the throbbing of the train's passing beneath my feet. Or is it the train? I stand in silence looking alternately at the sad little cross and the train. I look up and see the last box car coming. The one I did not want to wait for. If I don't hurry, the line of cars waiting behind the wall of the train will be clear to pass and I'll be stuck at the end of the parade, farther behind than if I had stopped when warned to.

Still, I stand. But just for a moment.

Then I race back to the car, rip open the back door and toss the prodigal hubcap onto the floor. I jump into the front seat and move off as fast as the snow and wind will allow, pulling away from the crossing where we'd met, the quick and the dead. The cross is lost to me now, its paleness swallowed by the washed-out landscape shining white in the wan winter sunlight.

High and Lifted Up

His doubt came creeping in as he knelt in the pre-dawn darkness of the sacristy. The room's only light came from a parking lot night-light coming through a small stained-glass window. This black dog had been visiting him more and more. *Why today, of all days?* Father Thomas Corrigan thought. Preparing for Easter Sunday Mass is a bad time for questioning the real presence of Christ. Not that there's any good time. But Easter?! He knew that the Missal proclaimed that in the "celebration of Mass... Christ is really present to the assembly gathered in his name: he is present in the person of the minister, in his own word, and indeed substantially and permanently under the Eucharistic elements."

It was that last part giving him trouble. *Christ is present in me, permanently under the Eucharistic elements? Me?*

His questioning had begun thirty years earlier, when he was in seminary. Until then he accepted the mystery of the real presence as that – a mystery. As a young boy he liked mysteries of all sorts, even religious ones. Even as a teenager, the thought of being a life-time servant of that great mystery held more allurement than the mystery of young women and sex, as strong a lures as they were. He knew in the deepest part of his soul that he wanted to be a priest. More than wanted. He felt compelled to bring the body and blood of Christ to the people of Christ. He longed to lead a congregation's joining itself to Jesus; their salvation purchased by the body and blood consumed during the Mass.

That longing took him to seminary where he studied to show himself approved, fit for Christ's service. But he found that all theological training quickly crowded out the mystery. He reveled in his studies, but he found academic postulations and theories filling his mind, body and soul, the rational leaving no room for the spiritual. Even while he thrived on the teachings of the Church's great theologians, he found their explanations robbing his once wonder-filled faith of any awe. Worst of all he found that he no longer believed that a priest's eucharistic prayer of thanksgiving changed the bread and wine into the body and blood of Christ. Especially when that priest was him. He was just a man, after all. A flawed man, at that. How could his prayers do anything when he doubted the very heart of faith. The only part of the Eucharist remaining true for him was his washing his hands as a sign of his desire to be cleansed within. That he knew he needed.

Still, he entered the priesthood. Kneeling on the prie-dieu that pre-dawn Easter, he wondered why. Even as he wondered, he knew a partial answer. Responsibility. He and the Church had invested in his education. He felt obligated; a sort of officer training candidate who was compelled to do his after-graduation hitch in God's army.

And he felt called – something he couldn't explain in the face of his doubt. Why would God call a man to minister a mystery he questioned?

Corrigan tried to make up for his doubts by being the best pastor a parish had ever known. He threw himself into his ministry, working himself so ragged that he collapsed in his bed every night, too tired to think, to wonder, to doubt. He spent hours on his homilies. He attended every program or sporting event featuring his parish's children that he could. He visited frequently and regularly – at the hospital, nursing homes, and with shut-ins. He took the mystery to those who couldn't come to it. Catechumens and pensioners alike loved him. He loved them. He loved the priesthood. He loved Jesus. He just doubted the real presence.

It's a good thing nobody can hear this, he thought, smoothing the sleeves of his alb, alone in the half-darkness. *I hope it's not contagious. I'd especially hate to infect Donnie with this disease.*

Donnie was the altar boy who most regularly helped Corrigan with the Mass. Corrigan often noticed Donnie looking up at him with the same hope-filled, wondering eyes that Corrigan had had as a boy. But Donnie wasn't there that morning. He was home sick. He had fallen ill at the conclusion of the Good Friday service. Corrigan saw the boy stumble as they left the altar. Reaching the back of the sanctuary on Friday, he had turned the boy around and seen that he was flushed and sweating.

"You're burning up, so," said Corrigan, feeling the boy's forehead. "Have your mother take you straight home." Donnie's mother called later. She said that Donnie's fever was high, and he was listless. He just wanted to sleep. The doctor was supposed to make a rare house call. "I hope it's just some pre-teen boy thing," she said, worry lining her voice. She wondered "could Father please make other arrangements for an altar boy for Sunday. And pray for my son?"

He'd prayed for Donnie, but found no other altar boys or girls to fill in. He'd tried but gotten no firm commitments. It was spring break and many of his students and their families were in Florida for the holidays. *What a way to spend Holy Week. These days,* he thought, *commitment is just a word to most people. Some days I doubt their faith.* His face burned with guilt. *Almost as much as I do mine. Why should I wonder at other peoples' faith when I wonder about my own?*

Here he knelt on the holiest day of the Christian calendar, dismayed by doubt. "Dear Jesus, son of the Blessed Mother, grant me release from the worry. Help me administer the sacrament in a way worthy to your name. Forgive my sin. In the name of the Father, the Son, and the Holy Spirit," he prayed. He stood to begin preparing the elements. It was then he heard a rustling.

Turning, he saw a young priest entering the sacristy. *Who is he and what is he doing here,* Corrigan thought, heading for the wardrobe holding his chasubles. Picking out his best white one his heart skipped and almost stopped. *Could he be one of the young priests who spied for the bishop? Had word gotten out of his doubt? How could it? He had never told anybody about his feelings.*

The young priest approaching him did not fit Corrigan's stereotype of a spy. This fellow was in his mid-thirties, with clear eyes and a short beard. He smiled disarmingly. Perhaps that's what makes him a good spy, Corrigan thought, donning the chasuble. He wouldn't be tricked into revealing anything. He had kept his doubt to himself these many years; he could keep it another hour. The young priest would find nothing out from him.

"Hello, Father Corrigan," the young man said, voice light and clean. It almost rang in the stillness of the sacristy.

"Lo," Corrigan grunted, not asking the young man's name. He didn't want to give him any entrance for his episcopal espionage. Corrigan stepped over to the chest containing his stoles, opened a drawer, and chose a white one matching his chasuble.

"May I be of some assistance?" the young priest asked, oh so helpfully. Corrigan couldn't detect a hint of sarcasm or obsequiousness in his tone.

Corrigan was momentarily stumped. Did he say "yes?" Some assistance would be nice with Donnie out sick. But that would allow the spy an opening. Corrigan decided he needed no help. *May as well be defrocked for discourtesy as disbelief,* he reasoned. "No, thanks," he said curtly, putting on the stole and shutting the drawer.

"Fine," the young man replied, unperturbed. "Do you mind if I sit here?" He pulled up a chair as Corrigan went to the cabinet holding the cruets for the water and wine. He got them out and set them on top of the stole chest. Then he went and got the water and wine, all the while keeping his back to the stranger. He worked in silence until the young priest broke it, saying, "I love Easter morning, don't you, Father?"

"It's okay," said Corrigan, knowing that he didn't love it, didn't love it at all. Well, he didn't hate it. It just made him even more uneasy about his doubt. He sensed the young man knew he felt that way. He worried that the priest's question was just the opening gambit in the inquisitional chess game that was to come.

"It's the finest day of the Christian calendar," the young priest went on, ignoring Corrigan's curtness. "Not because that's the appropriate answer for a priest," he chuckled, softly, "but because it really is. It is better than Christmas anytime."

"How so?" Corrigan grumped, slightly intrigued. He carefully filled the cruets. *Where is he going with this?*

"Well, you see, at Christmas," said the young priest, "the focus is on a baby in a manger. That's all he is – a cute, cuddly baby in a crèche, surrounded by plaster saints that never change, never age, and rarely make a difference. It's a tale too familiar from two thousand years of telling. But Easter... now that's different."

"Hardly," scoffed Corrigan, returning the water and wine to their cabinet. "We've been telling that story for two thousand years, too."

"True, true," agreed the young man. "But this story is not as tidy as the Christmas story. Easter is full of passion, power, blood, bread and spirit. Abandonment. Lust. Lying. Murder. It's a tale too messy to be sanitized. There's no making it safe. It is a story of Bethlehem's babe breaking bread and sharing wine and then being flailed and crowned with thorns. Raised high on a cross and slammed down into the dirt. He hangs there naked, in agony, his mother crying and soldiers gambling for his clothes."

Instead of growing light with the approaching dawn, the room seemed to fill with blackness and despair as the young man spoke. The darkness mirrored Corrigan's doubt, which intensified with the telling. Finally, when it seemed it couldn't grow any darker, the young priest spoke again.

"But then comes the morning we call Easter. The first person to encounter the mystery is Mary. Brokenhearted she has made her way to the tomb. In disbelief she sees the stone rolled away. She fails to remember Jesus' teaching. Instead, she fears that someone has stolen the body. Her belief is small, but her love is great. She goes to tell the others and then returns to the tomb. She stands there weeping, her soul pouring out."

Corrigan is transferring the host into the ciborium and notices that his heart is tendered by Mary's story. A story he's heard and told thousands of times.

"Then Jesus appears. She doesn't know who he is; thinks he must be the gardener. She knows him only when he speaks a single word. 'Mary,' he says. When he speaks her name, she knows it is him, body and blood together and real in her presence. You see, Easter is not about lack of doubt; it is about the one who calls us each by name. He calls us by name, Thomas. All because of the body and the blood."

Hearing those words, Corrigan's heart burned within him. Silence swelled, filling the sacristy. Corrigan stood at the shelf, before the water, wine, and host, his heart lighter, his mind less troubled, but weeping, nonetheless. Doubt didn't matter at this moment. The entire room seemed a sacrament, each moment a prayer. It was enough. It was a mystery.

He turned to the young priest, but he wasn't there. Instead, there sat Donnie, dressed and ready to do his duty.

"Are you okay, Father?" Donnie asked, staring at Corrigan's red eyes and tear-streaked face? "I got here in time, didn't I? I didn't think I would. I was pretty sick. But I woke up early and felt okay. Mom and Dad were still asleep, so I got dressed as quiet as I could and beat it on down here. I'm not too late, am I?"

"Where is he?" Corrigan stuttered, eyes darting around the room.

"Where's who?" asked Donnie, looking around, trying to see what the priest was looking for.

"The young priest I was talking to," Corrigan said.

"I didn't see any priest," said Donnie. "You were the only one here when I got here."

"But... but..." said Corrigan, turning back to the altar. There sat the cruets and ciborium glowing, illuminated by the Easter morning sunlight shining through the stained glass. He picked up the ciborium to move it into the sanctuary. It was then he noticed that, though removed from the spot where the sunbeam fell, it still radiated soft, golden light.

"Look at that," said Donnie, his eyes bright with wonder. "It's still glowing. How can that be?"

Corrigan stood rooted in place, not speaking. Finally, he spoke softly, "It's a mystery to me."

Mexico

Luke Henry passed away in January 1976. The years of smoking Camels had finally caught up with him. In the early '70s he was diagnosed with emphysema and by 1973 he was tethered by a tube to an oxygen tank. Though he couldn't smoke after that, he missed the smell of burning tobacco and drawing it in. And the feel of a pack in his shirt pocket and a single Camel between his fingers.

Luke grew thin to the point of gauntness and spent most of his time in the corner of the sofa where he'd been sitting when his brother Shirl called about their brother Farley's death almost twenty years earlier. He sat there reading a large print Bible or the morning *Citizen-Journal* or practicing his newly acquired art of needlepoint. And just thinking. And thinking.

On the nicest of days, he rested in a wicker glider on the porch under its blue painted ceiling. He sat so still that the birds and squirrels got used to his presence. He took peanuts out with him and held them still between his thumb and index finger. A cardinal, his favorite bird, would come and peck the peanut out of his fingers and crack it open on the porch floor. That brought Luke joy.

Luke continued to fade. Something that constantly amazed him. He didn't feel any older. He did feel betrayed by his body. Eventually, its betrayal was complete. One snow-covered cold morning, Lillian went to check on him. Luke was sitting in his usual place on the sofa, the newspaper flat on his lap, and not breathing. He was buried three days later up in Oak Grove Cemetery, next to his brothers Farley and Shirl who were already resting there under their blankets of snow.

As Christmas approached that year, Esther phoned Luke Junior. They had both moved from Columbus after they married. "It's not right for Mother to be alone on the first Christmas after Daddy," Esther told him.

"You're right," Luke Junior agreed. "Let's take the kids, go home and surprise her. It will be the first time we've been together on Christmas in ten years."

They made plans to meet outside of town and drive to the family home. They'd bring dinner and presents and celebrate Christmas in the white house on Richardson Avenue where they'd had their childhood holidays. As they came through the front door of their old home, Mrs. Henry's eyes lit up with joy and appreciation. Luke Junior noticed that the scent of smoked Camels still hung heavy in the room.

Both her children noticed something different about their mother but couldn't quite figure out what. That afternoon, when Esther and Mrs. Henry were washing dishes, Esther looked up from the sink and said, "I know. I know. You've done something with your hair."

Mrs. Henry nodded, color flooding her cheeks. "I changed to a younger style and put a rinse on," she said shyly.

Luke Junior's wife, Rita, looked up from sweeping the kitchen floor and asked, "Where are your glasses?"

"You may as well know," said Mrs. Henry, "I now wear contact lenses. And that's not all. I visited the cosmetics department at Lazarus and had a consultation. I now am the proud owner of a shelf full of make-up. Even this pantsuit is new. I guess I have become a vain old woman."

Esther and Rita smiled and hugged Mrs. Henry.

Just then there came a knock on the door. Luke Junior hollered in from his father's seat on the living room sofa, "I'll get it." He made his way to the wood and glass front door and opened it. There stood three kids, who jumped back in surprise. "Who'r you?" the oldest one demanded.

"What do you mean, 'who am I?'" Luke Junior answered gruffly. "I'm Luke Henry."

"Can't be. Mr. Henry's dead."

"In Heaven," said the little girl.

"Well, you're right there," Luke Junior replied a little gentler. "I mean, I'm Luke Henry Junior. Mr. Henry's son."

"Oh," said the oldest boy. The youngest boy still standing slight behind the older boy. "I guess that's okay then."

"Glad you approve," said Luke Junior with a bit of a smile. "Why are you here?" He noticed that their clothes looked more than a bit worn.

"We come to see Mrs. Henry," the oldest proclaimed.

"We got a present for her," said the girl.

The littlest boy stepped out from around the older boy and held out a small package wrapped in the color Sunday comic pages.

Just then Mrs. Henry appeared behind her son and smiled. Her face lit up and nudging Luke Junior aside said, "Come in, children, come in." Then she yelled upstairs to her grandchildren, "Come down. There are some people I want you to meet."

The grandchildren trooped down, though they would have rather stayed upstairs watching television and playing board games.

"I want you to meet some friends of mine," said Mrs. Henry happily. "This is Tommy, Maria, and Lamont. They live here on Richardson Avenue and come to a little Bible class I hold here every Tuesday after school." She introduced her grandchildren to the avenue kids before ushering them all into the kitchen for cookies and milk. Soon the kids, all about the same ages, were talking to each other. Tommy and Mark, her oldest grandson, talked about the next day's NFL playoff games, while the younger kids played "Skunk" around the kitchen table, trying to get points and avoid having their dice throw come up with a picture of a skunk. Mrs. Henry pulled up a chair and contentedly watched them, smiling.

After a while the avenue kids said they needed to be going home. "Oh, but first we have a present for you," said Tommy. Lamont pulled out the comic paper wrapped gift and handed it to Mrs. Henry.

"Well, good heavens," she exclaimed. "A present for me? How thoughtful. Let's go into the living room. I have something there for each of you, too."

In the living room she knelt close to the tree and pulled out a nicely wrapped package for each of the three avenue kids. They tore into the wrapping paper. A new pair of blue jeans for Tommy, a dress for Maria, and a warm flannel shirt, for Lamont. They held up their gifts to show everybody, with expressions of thanks. Mrs. Henry looked at her grandchildren and said, "You'll get your presents when we open our gifts in a little while."

Lamont stood up and came over to the easy chair where Mrs. Henry sat. "This is for you," he said, holding out their present. "It ain't much," said Tommy quietly. Marie added, "But all us kids in the Bible group chipped in."

"You mean there's more than just you three?" asked Luke Junior.

"Sure is," replied Tommy. "Sometimes there's ten or twelve of us here."

Mrs. Henry nodded in agreement.

Luke Junior sighed.

Mrs. Henry carefully unwrapped the comic paper. "Oh, look," she exclaimed, "some of my favorites are on here! 'Blondie,' 'Gasoline Alley,' 'Snuffy Smith,' and 'Peanuts.' How nice of you to share them with me." Then she held up a small, black Bible covered in imitation leather. "A new Bible," she said. "It's just what I needed."

"Mom, don't you have..." started Luke Junior before Rita, seated next to him on the sofa, elbowed him in the ribs and shot him a look.

"We got it down at Wagner's Five and Dime on Sullivant Avenue," said Lamont. "Y' know, right next to the Ritz Movie House."

"It is just perfect," smiled Mrs. Henry. "Perfect."

"Well, we gotta go now," said Tommy and the kids made their way to the front door and then out into the cold December late afternoon. At the bottom of the steps, they turned and waved. Mrs. Henry threw them kisses. Only Tommy looked a bit embarrassed.

Closing the door, she crossed the room and returned to her chair, picking up the small Bible and smiling at it.

"I didn't know you were teaching a Bible class here," said Esther.

"Me, neither," said Luke Junior. "I'm not sure I approve. Here you are elderly, living alone, and these ragamuffins coming in here. They might be stealing you blind."

"Luke Junior," she huffed. "I'm ashamed of you. To think such a thing. And so what? Even if they were, perhaps they need it. And I don't. Didn't Jesus himself tell us to show love to the least of these? That's what I'm doing. A warm room, fresh baked cookies, cold milk or hot cocoa, and a little Bible never hurt anyone. It may even help them." She paused. "I know it helps me," she said softly.

"Well, I don't know. I mean, I guess I don't know you like I thought I did," he replied. "I just heard about the contact lenses and make-up."

Mrs. Henry looked at her son and said, "Actually, there's a lot you don't know about your mother."

"Such as," asked Esther.

Mrs. Henry looked at her children and their spouses and said, "For instance, I have always thought of myself as an independent woman. Yes," she continued, "I loved your father and depended on him, but I mean in comparison to my mother. I am a woman of the twentieth century, unlike your grandmother who fit the model image of a late-nineteenth century wife."

She paused for breath. "For example, did you know I was an excellent student?"

"Yes, Mom," said Luke Junior, "you certainly told me enough times when report cards came out."

"Well, did you know that I defied your grandfather who wanted me to marry soon after graduating from high school? Instead, I went to Columbus Bible College for one year. The next summer I was off on a mission trip to Belize with some of my classmates."

"Mother Henry, really?" exclaimed Rita. "I had no idea."

"After I got back, I still wasn't ready to get married. For one, none of the boys – and they seemed like boys to me – at church held the slightest interest for me. So, I took a job as a salesclerk at the F. & R. Lazarus store downtown. I rode a streetcar, even at night, by myself. No chaperone. Father wasn't happy."

She went on to tell them how it was on the streetcar that she'd met Mr. Henry who found himself enchanted by her handsome looks and quick-silver wit. He followed her home, introduced himself to her parents and asked permission to court her. Mrs. Henry's father refused but Mr. Henry was determined. He made sure he rode the streetcar often so that he could talk to the young salesclerk. She defied her father once again and started seeing the slightly older railroad man. He kept riding the streetcar and even accompanied her to the Bible study she taught in a tenement in the Bottoms. And won her heart.

"He was a man, not a boy," said Mrs. Henry. "I was ready for marriage then. Now it's time for presents. Call the children down, won't you?"

After the presents had been unwrapped and exclaimed over, the grandchildren took one of the board games they'd received and headed for the kitchen table to try it out. Mrs. Henry stood up and started to gather the torn wrapping paper and bows.

"Sit down, Mom, and relax," Esther said. "Rita and I'll take care of this mess." For once Mrs. Henry didn't protest.

Luke Junior got up and stretched. "I need a smoke. I'll be right back." He went outside on the porch and lit a Camel. Esther's husband, Ralph, joined him. The women could see the red tips of the cigarettes in the gathering gloom as the day faded.

When the men came back in, Luke Junior grumped, "The old neighborhood sure has changed. Lots of the houses need paint. Or new roofs. Cars are parked solid down both sides of the street. There's even a car parked right in front of your house."

"Do you mean that silver Chevrolet Chevette?" asked Mrs. Henry.

"I guess that's what it is," answered Luke Junior. "Do you know who's it is?"

"That I do," replied Mrs. Henry. "It is mine. I took lessons from the Triple-A. I passed my driver's test on the first try. A perfect 100," she boasted, pulling her flimsy paper license from her purse sitting on the end table. "Lillian Shields Henry" read the line immediately under State of Ohio.

"That's wonderful, Mother," Esther said.

"We're so proud of you," added Rita.

Luke Junior didn't say anything. Nor did Ralph.

Later, after the grandchildren vanished upstairs to watch television in Mrs. Henry's bedroom, the adults sat around reliving the day and days past. Luke Junior looked out the front windows to the street.

"It's supposed to snow tonight," he said in a voice that brought Mr. Henry to mind. "Want me to put the car in the garage for you?"

"Yes, thank you, son," Mrs. Henry replied. "That would be nice. The keys are in my purse. The automatic garage door opener is clipped to the sun visor." She wondered what he would think of the boxes marked "boy's clothing" or "girl's clothing" resting on the back seat and the AAA TripTik to Matamoras, Mexico, in the console above the shifter.

Then she smiled and thought of the places she would go.

Another Trip to Amity

She could imagine him fuming. She could hear the engine revving and imagined him thinking about leaving without her. *As if that would ever happen*, she thought and continued fixing her hair. *There'd be hell to pay if he did.*

Still, she moved quickly from the downstairs half-bath, through the kitchen and out into the garage. Then she remembered she forgot her make-up, rushed through the house, grabbed her mascara and lipstick and stuffed them into her purse while going through the garage. She climbed into the car and told him, "I'll put my face on while we drive. That way you can get going."

He grunted, put the car in reverse, and backed quickly out the driveway. He almost ran over the neighbor's cat that was walking across the concrete. He tore down the street and screeched around the corner. She held tight to the door handle. "We've plenty of time," she said, while thinking, *if he drives like this the whole way I'll never be able to put on lipstick, let alone mascara. I'd put an eye out.* Then she wondered if he remembered to put the garage door down. He often forgot to do that when he was in a snit and rushing to get somewhere.

"So, you say," he snapped at her. "You always say that when you're making us run late." He was almost right about that. She had made them run late many times. Late by his standards, that is. He always wanted to be at least fifteen to twenty minutes early to everything. Even if it meant that they sometimes arrived so early they had to wait in the car for a little while. Most of the time she shrugged it off. She and their daughters laughed about "Dad-time." If he said they needed to be there by 9:10 that meant it started at 9:30. She did love him. She remembered meeting him while she was working with a youth group's money-making breakfast. He was obviously interested. She was a little slower falling for him. She loved him this moment, too, though she was as aggravated as hell with him.

So, she said, "Sorry," though she looked out the side window, looking out her window, watching the houses rush by.

"Sorry doesn't make up the time we've lost. The service starts at 10:30, it's 9:45 now, we've got 30 miles of mostly two-lane to cover and I told you I wanted to leave at 9:30." His ears turned as red as his cheeks as impatience reached them.

"I'm sorry," she said again to the window. May as well speak to the window as him. He obviously wasn't listening.

"Yes, you've been sorry for thirty years now," he tore on. "Instead of being sorry I wish you'd just get ready on schedule. I'd like you to have a little respect for my feelings, for the way I want to get places on time. It may not seem like much to you, but most people like their guest minister to be there when worship starts."

"I thought the service started at 11:00," she said softly. "I thought we had plenty of time."

"Well, it doesn't. It starts at 10:30 and that's why I kept asking if you were ready. But no, you just had to..."

"Sorry."

That was the last spoken by either of them. The only sound was the wind whistling by the windshield and the thoughts inside her head. *What made him this way?* she wondered, as she'd been wondering for years. *He can be so kind and loving and fun. Until one of these snits comes on him. Then, Mr. Personality Change. Maybe it had something to do with being passed over for assistant to the bishop. He'd really been counting on that. And he wasn't getting any younger.* The sun warmed the car, and he cracked his window. She wished he'd turn on the a/c. Maybe it would calm him. At the very least it would cool her.

"Do you want to turn on the air conditioner?" she asked.

"No, I do not," he growled.

Hmmm, he must be really mad. She knew that when he got that way there was no placating him. Not until it worked itself out. He seemed to almost enjoy being pissed. *So sad,* she thought. *What a waste of energy. Especially on a nice Sunday morning, perfect for enjoying the growing crops and tidy farmsteads along the way.* So that's what she did. Silently contemplated the beauty spreading out to the far Iowa horizons.

Damn! He muttered. She looked at the clock on the dashboard. 10:32.

"What?" she asked. He glared at her. She imagined him thinking they were late and that it was all her fault. As if a few minutes mattered.

The outskirts of a small town loomed out of the haze ahead. She assumed it was Amity. The night before, he'd pulled the Iowa roadmap out of the car's glovebox and memorized their route, as he always did before any trip. Sure enough "Amity, population 400" read the sign they passed, slowing as a white frame church surrounded by sedans and pickup trucks filled their windshield. He pulled into the lot, found an empty spot, and parked. He jumped out, yanked open the back door, grabbed his robe off the hanger and began putting it on.

Finally having a car that wasn't bouncing down a two-lane road, she started putting lipstick on. He reached in the car, grabbed his Bible and sermon notebook off the back seat, slammed the car door, and left her sitting in the front seat. He looked at his watch as he stormed across the parking lot, stoles flapping behind him, and raced up the church steps.

She put on mascara. And then she just sat. One of them needed to be calm. So, she looked over the plain white church. It was pleasant looking and fit well with its surroundings. She couldn't see the whole structure but noticed that the front windows were just clear glass. No stained-glass depictions of Bible scenes. *That's nice,* she thought. *You'd be able to sit and look out the window and nature around you. And how the sunlight must fill that room.* She sighed and decided to stretch her legs.

A small graveyard was there so she walked through it. Like the church building, it was neat and trim. She looked at some of the names on the gravestones. She noticed a dearth of "sons" names like Andersons, Johnsons, Petersons, and Swensons found in most Lutheran graveyards in that part of the state. Instead, there was an abundance of Cadburys, Hinshaws, Lindleys, and Newlins. *They must have come from the east,* she thought, *not immigrated from Scandinavia.*

She finally decided to go in. She walked up the steps, accepted a bulletin from an usher, and made her way to a pew, where she could sit alone. It wasn't hard to find one. The building was far from crowded. She bowed her head. She took some time to pray. To pray for more patience with her impatient husband. To better honor his urgent need to be early instead of her uncomfortableness with always being too early. She listened to the familiar tune of Martin Luther's "From Depths of Woe I Cry to Thee" the organist was playing. The opening words reflected what was in her heart:

From depths of woe I cry to thee,
Lord, hear me, I implore thee.
Bend down thy gracious ear to me,
my prayer let come before thee.

Lord, hear my prayer, she thought earnestly. She looked up and scanned the bulletin, looking for what other good Lutheran hymns they'd be singing. Hopefully, something not "A Mighty Fortress Is Our God" or any other heavy Luther tunes. New. As she looked, she saw that all the other hymn titles were unfamiliar to her. As was the order of worship, too.

She looked at the header of the bulletin. "Amity Friends Church (Quaker)" she read with alarm. Oh my! They were in the wrong church. The wrong church! She had to stifle a snicker. All this rushing and they ended up in the wrong place. She read more of the bulletin, trying not to smile. "Howard Mason, Pastor," it announced. She had to squeeze her eyes shut and try not to laugh. So that must be the fellow on the platform next to him. But her amusement began to wane as she thought of the embarrassment her husband was going to feel when he found out.

She looked up. He was looking at her. His eyes were soft. Ah, the anger had passed, and he was back to himself. That almost made what had happened worse.

She looked him in the eye and mouthed her message. She thought he might get what she was not saying aloud. Over the years they had learned to read each other's lips. He looked puzzled.

She tried again. Very slowly. He looked back at her and shrugged his shoulders. A few people around her looked at her and then him, following the silent interchange. She mouthed her message with even more exaggerated movements. He leaned forward in the pulpit chair, as if getting closer might help convey her silent words to him. Nothing. More people were watching them now. Her husband leaned closer, so much so that he almost fell out of the chair. She heard a couple of quiet chuckles. She sighed, closed her eyes, grabbed the back of the pew in front of her, stood up and spoke.

"We're in the wrong church."

She saw him sit back, stunned. He turned to the man she knew was the Quaker minister, who nodded in confirmation. Face burning brightly, he stood up straight, and with head high, he stepped down off the platform, and walked down the main aisle. He stopped next to her, paused by his wife, offered his arm, and together they went out of the building.

Going down the front steps, she handed him her bulletin. "Amity Friends Church (Quaker)" he read. A young man, hustling up the walkway toward them looked at the woman and her robed escort. "Excuse me," she said, "could you tell us where the Amity Lutheran Church is?"

"Sure," said the man, pointing "It's a mile and a half that ways out T-66."

"Thank you," she said, leading her husband to the sedan. She started rummaging in her purse, but he placed his hand over hers, stopping her. He walked her around to her side of the car, unzipped his robe, fished his keys out of his pocket, unlocked her door and helped her in.

Then he walked around the car and climbed in his side. Ten forty-seven said the dashboard clock. "That was the longest 7 minutes of my life," he said.

He started the car, put it in gear, backed out of the lot, and headed west.

"We may as well go on out there. I'll apologize for going to the wrong church." Then he snickered. She finally chuckled out loud. Soon a summer storm of laughter rained down on them so hard that he had to slow down because he was having trouble keeping the car on the road. A few minutes later they zigged into a lot next to a fine red brick church with a bright white steeple.

They parked next to a sign that said, "Amity Lutheran Church, Sunday School 10:00 a.m., Worship 11:00 a.m."

Ten fifty-three read the dashboard clock. They looked at the clock, the sign, each other and started giggling again. There was much she wanted to say. And he had some things to say, too. But they just sat and laughed. Cars and pickups joined theirs in the lot. Many congregants stared at them; two middle-aged folks, one in a black robe replete with stoles, laughing so hard their car shook.

At 11:05 they were alone in the parking lot. He wiped his eyes, climbed out of the car, zipped his robe, straightened his stoles, and picked up his Bible and sermon notes. Then he walked around the car, opened his wife's door, took her arm and headed slowly for the church.

About Brent

J. Brent Bill is a Quaker minister, author, retreat leader, conservationist, and photographer. He has authored many books, articles, and fiction pieces and teaches writing at graduate school level and in adult continuing education courses. Brent holds degrees from Wilmington College and in Quaker Studies from Earlham School of Religion (a Quaker theological school).

He lives on Ploughshares Farm, forty acres of former Indiana farmland that is being restored to tall grass prairie and native Indiana hardwood forest.

In addition to writing, Brent also enjoys leading workshops and speaking. Some of his most popular workshops are:

"Life Lessons from A Bad Quaker" is a light-hearted, but serious, workshop for anyone who is bad at being good. With whimsy, humor, and wisdom, workshop participants will explore how to live a life that is simple yet satisfying, peaceful yet strong.

"Writing from the Heart: Telling Your Soul's Stories" is for those who want to write with soulful and heartfelt language to unlock their innermost stories.

"Being Quiet: The Practice of Holy Silence" is based on Quaker silence and teaches how to be quiet and still in our souls amid the clamor of everyday life.

If you would like more information about Brent's writing, his workshops and retreats, or would like to contact him about other speaking engagements, you can reach him through his website at www.brentbill.com or via e-mail at brentbil@brentbill.com.

ROUNDFIRE
BOOKS

FICTION

Historical fiction that lives

Put simply, we publish great stories. Whether it's literary or popular, a gentle tale or a pulsating thriller, the connecting theme in all Roundfire fiction titles is that once you pick them up you won't want to put them down.
If you have enjoyed this book, why not tell other readers by posting a review on your preferred book site.

Recent bestsellers from Roundfire are:

The Bookseller's Sonnets
Andi Rosenthal
The Bookseller's Sonnets intertwines three love stories with a
tale of religious identity and mystery spanning five hundred
years and three countries.
Paperback: 978-1-84694-342-3 ebook: 978-184694-626-4

Birds of the Nile
An Egyptian Adventure
N.E. David
Ex-diplomat Michael Blake wanted a quiet birding trip up the
Nile – he wasn't expecting a revolution.
Paperback: 978-1-78279-158-4 ebook: 978-1-78279-157-7

Blood Profit$
The Lithium Conspiracy
J. Victor Tomaszek, James N. Patrick, Sr.
The blood of the many for the profits of the few... *Blood Profit$*
will take you into the cigar-smoke-filled room where American
policy and laws are really made.
Paperback: 978-1-78279-483-7 ebook: 978-1-78279-277-2

The Burden
A Family Saga
N.E. David
Frank will do anything to keep his mother and father
apart. But he's carrying baggage – and it might just weigh
him down ...
Paperback: 978-1-78279-936-8 ebook: 978-1-78279-937-5

The Cause
Roderick Vincent
The second American Revolution will be a fire lit from
an internal spark.
Paperback: 978-1-78279-763-0 ebook: 978-1-78279-762-3

Don't Drink and Fly
The Story of Bernice O'Hanlon: Part One
Cathie Devitt
Bernice is a witch living in Glasgow. She loses her way in her
life and wanders off the beaten track looking for the garden of
enlightenment.
Paperback: 978-1-78279-016-7 ebook: 978-1-78279-015-0

Gag
Melissa Unger
One rainy afternoon in a Brooklyn diner, Peter Howland
punctures an egg with his fork. Repulsed, Peter pushes the
plate away and never eats again.
Paperback: 978-1-78279-564-3 ebook: 978-1-78279-563-6

The Master Yeshua
The Undiscovered Gospel of Joseph
Joyce Luck
Jesus is not who you think he is. The year is 75 CE. Joseph
ben Jude is frail and ailing, but he has a prophecy to fulfi l ...
Paperback: 978-1-78279-974-0 ebook: 978-1-78279-975-7

On the Far Side, There's a Boy
Paula Coston
Martine Haslett, a thirty-something 1980s woman, plays hard on the fringes of the London drag club scene until one night which prompts her to sign up to a charity. She writes to a young Sri Lankan boy, with consequences far and long.
Paperback: 978-1-78279-574-2 ebook: 978-1-78279-573-5

Tuareg
Alberto Vazquez-Figueroa
With over 5 million copies sold worldwide, *Tuareg* is a classic adventure story from best-selling author Alberto Vazquez-Figueroa, about honour, revenge and a clash of cultures.
Paperback: 978-1-84694-192-4

Readers of ebooks can buy or view any of these bestsellers by clicking on the live link in the title. Most titles are published in paperback and as an ebook. Paperbacks are available in traditional bookshops. Both print and ebook formats are available online.

Find more titles and sign up to our readers' newsletter at
http://www.johnhuntpublishing.com/fiction

Follow us on Facebook at https://www.facebook.com/
JHPfiction and Twitter at https://twitter.com/JHPFiction